A LOT OF

CK

Elise Lowe

SOCCIONES

ISBN: 9781980611233

Cover design & formatting by Socciones Editoria Digitale
www.socciones.co.uk

For Elliot, Amani and James, who were there at the beginning
and made it fun to keep going.

With special thanks to Nat Brownstein for your enthusiasm, Mum for your babysitting, Andrew, Lisa, Dan, and my other proofreaders (already mentioned), and to my old friends who know they are the best.

Chapter One

LAUREN and Ryan Liebman settle their taxi fare and make their way down the brightly lit pathway to the neo-Georgian block of flats they've called home for the past two years. The night porter welcomes them and asks Ryan if he needs a hand with the bags. Lauren thanks him, but says they'll be fine as she hears her husband curse her under his breath. He drags the matching Mulberry suitcases up two flights of stairs and when they reach their apartment he flings both the bags and himself through the front door without offering to carry Lauren over the threshold.

She is still feeling nauseous from the plane food, though she barely touched it, and only a little less angry than she was at check-in 17 hours ago when she was certain she could feel smoke blowing from her nostrils. They're the only couple she knows who failed to get upgraded on honeymoon and Lauren is in no doubt it's because Ryan refused to wear a suit.

She flicks on the lights and seeing him in colour gives a new lease of life to her simmering rage. He is unshaven, wearing old faded jeans and a grey hooded top emblazoned with luminous emoji faces. His thick brown hair is unstyled and greasy. "What you looking at?" he snaps, flopping onto the sofa.

"Nothing," she lies, still staring at his sweatshirt and wondering why her husband is incapable of making grown up fashion choices. "I just wish you'd made more of an effort."

He throws his head back. "The plane was full Lauren. It wouldn't have made a difference. Can you just let it go? Please. I'm getting sick of this."

"Well that makes two of us," Lauren yells as she storms into the bedroom, slamming the door behind her and thinking it should feel different now; she should feel like she's married, but she doesn't. The only difference is her surname, which has changed from Litchfield to Liebman, not even affording her a new initial. She growls loudly enough for Ryan to hear her. Then she walks slowly round the room, inspecting it as if it's yet another hotel she's just checked into; she notes the bed has been made by Agnus as instructed, dressed in the Egyptian cotton linen with the lace inlay Lauren bought especially for this new chapter in their lives. The small matching cushions have also been neatly arranged, although Lauren would have done it slightly differently.

She draws the curtains and catches a glimpse of her reflection in the dressing table mirror. She may have gained a few pounds since the wedding, but her body is still elegantly thin. Her skin is glowing with yesterday's sun, but her big brown eyes have lost their sparkle and dark circles are fighting their way through her carefully applied concealer. Her lips are dry and her straight black hair, usually full of volume, falls lankily around her shoulders, beaten into submission by the plane's overzealous air conditioning system.

Lauren briefly entertains the idea of calling Olivia and Julia, but quickly decides she is too tired. Instead, she makes her way to the bright, white, en-suite and runs a bath, determined to cleanse herself of any germs she may have picked up in the economy cabin. As she immerses herself in the warm, bubbly, water she feels the anger leave her body and she lies there, eyes closed, until her skin starts to crinkle. Afterwards, she slips into her silk negligee and delicately peels back the bed covers, which are delightfully fresh with newness. She falls asleep quickly, only waking momentarily when her husband lies down beside her; she turns her back on him before sinking back to sleep.

OLIVIA Johnson takes the industrial lift up to the third floor of a former furniture factory. Whenever she has company she brags about being the first to move into the property, which has only recently been reimagined as a collection of loft-style apartments. Tonight though, she is alone and as the music blaring from the bar below slowly fades, it is replaced by the ringing in her ears. As usual, she fights with the lock on her front door. When it finally gives way she kicks off her heels and heads straight for the L-shaped, aubergine sofa, which is currently serving as a centrepiece for her deliberately minimalist living space. (Her friends would argue her minimalism is greatly compromised by the huge amount of mess on the floor.) Sitting down, Olivia picks up a stale glass of water from the metal framed coffee table and gulps it down gratefully before fumbling around for her mobile phone, which is buzzing inside her bag. She eventually fishes it out, half reading a message from Benji, which looks like the usual, 'Did you get home ok?' She tosses the phone to the floor and lies down on the sofa, passing out moments later.

***

"Did I wake you?" Julia asks, when Olivia accidentally answers the phone, her intention being simply to make the ringing stop.

"Don't worry. I was just getting up," Olivia fibs, reaching for the almost empty glass of water on the coffee table. "Damn it," she mutters, as the final few drops do nothing to quench her thirst.

"I'm just checking we're still on for brunch," Julia continues, reminding Olivia of their arrangement, which she'd forgotten about.

"Sure," Olivia yawns. "I can be ready in an hour."

"Great!" Julia cries, with her usual high pitched enthusiasm. "You know, I think Lauren is back so maybe we should invite her too?"

Olivia groans. "No. Don't. I haven't got the energy for her today."

"She'll want to see us Liv. I'm calling her, okay?" Julia rarely sounds this authoritative and Olivia realises she's not really asking her permission.

"I've got to go. See you soon." Olivia drops the phone and runs to the bathroom, feeling last night's poison surge though her system; for the next 10 minutes she is certain she will die, but as always her body recovers with remarkable efficiency. A cold shower numbs the last of the pain, after which Olivia quickly dresses in dark skinny jeans and a low cut top. She touches up the makeup she never removes, reclaims her heels and dashes out her apartment.

JULIA Kettle is momentarily blinded by the light as she emerges from the underground. She doesn't remember the sun being this strong when she left her flat an hour ago and having failed to pack her sunglasses she squints all the way to the Hoxton Square café, which is just round the corner from Olivia's place. It would have been more convenient for Julia to meet Olivia somewhere in between the two of them, but she knows Olivia would have complained if she'd asked her to leave Zone One and possibly even cancelled at the last minute. This way she is guaranteed to see her friend and also guaranteed to eat a decent breakfast, which is almost more important.

Julia selects a booth by the window and squeezes in, wishing she hadn't worn shorts when her exposed thighs rub uncomfortably against the leather clad seating. There's no sign of Olivia so she orders herself a cappuccino, before pretending to study a sticky menu, already knowing she'll have the pancakes. She is thinking about which sauce to go for, salted caramel or maple syrup, when Olivia lands opposite her. "Sorry! Have you been here for ages?" she asks breathlessly.

"No, I just got here," Julia lies, not even looking at her watch because it would be ridiculous to expect Olivia to be on time. "I like your new haircut. Short really suits you."

Olivia gives her head a little shake. "Thanks. I wasn't sure, but you know it's easy."

Julia nods in agreement, unable to imagine having hair that does as it's supposed to. "It looks amazing. And I love the blonde. It's very bold."

Olivia flashes a knowing grin, then looks round the restaurant. "Is Lauren coming?"

"Yeah, she'll be late though. She's getting her nails done first. She said to order without her." Julia hands Olivia the menu. "Here you go. I'm starving!"

The waitress appears on cue and Julia requests her pancakes, opting for maple syrup once she's put on the spot, while Olivia chooses a fruit salad, demanding the chef remove half the fruit.

The waitress doesn't flinch and Julia realises her friend has done this many times before.

"Just give me one second." Olivia pulls her phone out her bag and starts frantically typing. "It's just this guy on Tinder," she explains, looking up. "It's actually becoming quite annoying. I think I need to come off it."

Julia laughs. Olivia has spent the last two years begging her to sign up and now even she's complaining about the dating App. "So what's news?" she asks, expecting Olivia to have a story for her because she usually does.

Olivia smiles and Julia spots the familiar twinkle in her eye. "I actually met someone in a bar last night."

"Wow. That is a turn out for the books. Where were you?" Julia leans forward, her interest piqued; she almost regrets staying in again.

"I was out round here with Benj and a few of his friends. There's that new place, Paradise. It's quite good you know. You should come next time. It's a cool crowd." Olivia stops talking as the surviving remnants of a fruit salad are placed in front of her. "Anyway, I was dancing and this guy came over, six foot, amazing dancer, really fit, you know."

Julia laughs at this description. "Name? Age? Job? I obviously need more."

She watches Olivia's eyes narrow like they always do when she's thinking really hard. "It was Michael or Mike. I'm not sure. I'm pretty certain he said he was 34. Used to run his own internet business, but that's kind of up in the air at the moment."

"Oh, how come?" Julia feels her stomach rumble with envy as Olivia picks at a strawberry.

"It's complicated." Olivia hesitates, a sombre expression creeping across her face. "He's been done for fraud or something. I mean, nothing serious, not a proper crime. It's so stupid though because he's got to do three months in jail, starting a week on Monday, so we're squeezing in a date on Thursday."

"Sounds like he's a keeper Liv! Are you planning to visit him behind bars?" Julia teases, already knowing the answer.

"As if!" Olivia cries. "It's just a bit of fun. Please don't tell Lauren though. You know what she's like." Julia nods obligingly, relieved to see her pancakes making their way towards her. Out of politeness she offers Olivia, who shakes her head and tells her she doesn't do carbs anymore.

"Your loss," Julia jokes, as she tucks in, savouring every syrup drenched mouthful.

"So how's work?" Olivia's tone is unambiguously judgemental. "Are they still exploiting you?"

Julia sighs, wishing she didn't have to have this conversation yet again. "It's the same. I haven't had a pay rise if that's what you mean? But, you know, it is good experience."

"Unbelievable!" Olivia howls, causing other people in the restaurant to pay attention to her too. "You should give them an ultimatum Julia: double your money or you're walking."

"Olivia it's a charity," Julia mumbles, trying to swallow the contents of her mouth. "That wouldn't go down well. I need to be careful. The last thing I want is to be unemployed and living back at my parents' place."

"Seriously Julia, loads of charities pay big bucks," Olivia insists, eyes wide with consternation. "They're taking advantage of you. You need to be tougher. How do you think the rest of us get ahead? If you don't ask, you don't get."

"I will. I will. I just need to find the right moment," Julia promises, seeing Lauren appear in her line of vision and thanking God for the timely intervention.

"Welcome back," Olivia hollers from her seat, while Julia jumps up to embrace her friend.

"You look stunning Lauren. We missed you," Julia chirps like a song bird. "Everyone's still talking about your wedding." Lauren beams with gratitude and slips into the booth beside Olivia, air kissing her hello.

"How was the moon?" Olivia asks, winking at Julia.

"I mean it was on another level," Lauren whines. "You wouldn't be able to imagine. If you ever get the chance to go to the Maldives…," she pauses briefly, almost certainly to remind her friends they'd need to meet someone first, "you know, you really should take it."

Julia watches Olivia indiscreetly roll her eyes, before turning her attention back to her phone.

OLIVIA hurriedly pays for her new snakeskin print handbag. Even as she hands over her credit card she isn't sure if she *really* wants it, but the security guard has started pulling down the shutters of the small boutique and in doing so has put her under *now or never* pressure to make the purchase. The noise of the shutters grates on her, reminding her of her hangover, which still hasn't completely subsided despite the late hour of the day. When she slides under her friends are waiting for her. "Girls I have to get going," she says apologetically. "I promised I'd go round to Benji's. He's cooking dinner for me."

"Ah Benji is so lovely," Julia coos with the kind of affection she'd have for a puppy. "Say hi from me."

"I should get going too," Lauren announces, looking at her watch, "but I'd love you guys to come round one night this week to see my wedding album. It's just arrived."

"Sounds great," Olivia says flatly, with no intention of making herself available.

"Can't wait," Julia echoes. "Let me know when!"

Olivia blows kisses at her friends and turns the corner, noticing how the East London streets remain full of people milling around pubs, pretending tomorrow isn't coming. She weaves her way through them, knowing within hours they'll be packing out the nearby bars and night clubs. She would gladly join them, were it not her night with Benji.

Benji lives just a few streets away from Olivia in a small apartment above an off licence, which as far as she can tell is predominantly frequented by underage drinkers. Just weeks before he began renting it, a couple of years back now, he was considering buying a place in the suburbs, but Olivia warned him he'd never see her again and he hasn't mentioned the idea since. She likes him being close. It feels right and like before…

Olivia and Benji had grown up on the same cul de sac and first met riding their bikes, before it was embarrassing for girls to be friendly with boys. Even later, when this was the case, they somehow ignored the rules. Benji would wait for Olivia on the bench outside her house, his braces gleaming in the sunshine. Once she was home from school they'd hang out together until dinner, playing on computer consoles or adopting false identities on early internet chat rooms (the internet was exciting back then). They ignored the homework they were supposed to be doing, and his parents, when they warned they would both fall behind. Olivia was too clever to fall behind, but Benji ended up with a tutor.

When she reaches Benji's apartment Olivia rings the buzzer for much longer than is necessary, knowing he can hear it and knowing the noise will annoy him. She eventually hears Benji thunder down the stairs and when he opens the door she can see he has been cooking because his hair has frizzed, which happens whenever he gets busy with the stove. He pulls her inside, enveloping her in a customary bear hug. The smell of whatever they are about to eat – it's always a roast of some description - has embedded itself in his clothing.

"I hope you're hungry Livvy. I've been slaving away." He pretends to mop the sweat from his brow.

"I'm excited," she laughs, following him up the stairs, noticing how his tracksuit bottoms are fraying at the edges and how his t-shirt has a large hole where the label used to be. This is not the Benji who gets dressed up for work or for restaurants and night clubs. This is the Benji only she knows, her Benji.

"I need about 10 more minutes in the kitchen," he says and Olivia leaves him to it, wandering into his bedroom, which is no less sparse than when he first moved in and personalised only by the three books on his bedside table and the neat pile of clothes living on a wooden chair in the corner. She sits on the end of the bed and takes off her heels, before crawling under the covers and falling asleep.

JULIA takes the Tube to Kings Cross, then switches to the Overground, which she prefers because even when busy it's somehow less of a suffocating experience. Her stop, Cricklewood, is right by the shops and she pops in, remembering she needs to buy a birthday card. She spins the display unit round until she finds what she is looking for, hardly believing her mother is going to be 70; over the years she's had to get used to having a mum who is older than everyone else's mum, but this doesn't make the impending birthday milestone any easier to digest. Julia's parents didn't expect to have her and she often gets the impression, 29 years on, they are still surprised by her very existence.

Card in hand, Julia crosses Cricklewood Lane and turns down a side street lined with unloved Victorian terraces. When she reaches her home, she is greeted by a stray cat who has taken a shine to her, perhaps because she leaves a bowl of milk out for him whenever she remembers. Julia pets the animal for some time before opening the front door, stepping over a pile of junk mail and heading up two flights of stairs to a studio flat nestled within the eaves of the house.

Although her flat is tiny by all accounts, Julia is quick to reassure anyone who shows concern that it has everything she needs, which is not very much at all. Her friends agree she has done a nice job, with the playful mix of art on the walls - mostly cheap prints she's picked up over the years - and the colourful woven rug, a cast off from her parents, she's placed in the centre of her living and sleeping area.

She sits on her bed intending to write her mother's card, but gets distracted when she spots the photograph resting on the window sill. It was taken at Lauren's 18th birthday party, which at the time felt like the most important event Julia would ever attend, but has since been surpassed by Lauren's wedding. In the photo Julia is sandwiched between her two best friends, looking better than usual because Lauren insisted she have her hair professionally blow-dried. It's by far and away the most flattering photo she has of herself and the only one to be publicly displayed outside of her parents' home. (In the name of damage limitation she has always refused to go on Facebook and done her best to avoid being photographed in general). Lauren, who is naturally photogenic, is doing an excellent job of pretending to have a good time - Julia remembers how she cried in the toilets after Robert, her boyfriend of just a few weeks, dumped her at the start of the night - while Olivia is posing provocatively for the camera, winding up Benji who was charged with taking the picture. He'd been the one to carry Olivia home that night and the next day he confessed to Julia he'd stayed in her room until morning just to make sure she didn't choke on her own vomit. It was difficult, almost impossible, to be around Olivia that year, and Julia couldn't help but blame her friend's parents for the way in which they separated.

LAUREN rants wildly as she picks up Ryan's worn boxer shorts from the bedroom floor and deposits them in the wash basket. It was only yesterday when she calmly explained how this kind of thoughtless behaviour made her feel disrespected; though her husband pretended to listen, she now realises her message fell on deaf ears. Before she can wash her hands, Lauren's mother rings to invite them both over for dinner and Lauren accepts the invitation without asking Ryan.

When she heads into the living room she finds her husband slumped on the sofa watching sport. She stands directly in front of him to block his view of the television, a huge flat screen he'd insisted upon even though she'd argued it was ridiculous given the modest size of the room. "Ryan we're going to my mum's tonight," she informs him. "Please shave before we leave."

"I can't do tonight Lauren. I'm busy," he grunts, shifting his position so he can still focus on the screen as she moves once again to block him.

"What are you talking about? We don't have any plans," she says crossly, wondering why, if he did have plans, he couldn't have spent 30 seconds updating their shared diary.

"I've got stuff to do. Go without me." He lets out a yawn, signalling for her to move out of the way, but she doesn't budge.

"What stuff? My mum will be upset." She leans forward, snatching the remote control which has been resting beside him on the sofa and turns off the television.

"What the hell d'you do that for?" he yells, his face reddening. "I'm watching the football."

"And I'm trying to talk to you," she shouts back, feeling her pulse race as she hides the device behind her back. "I want you to come tonight."

He stands up; she imagines this is his animalistic attempt to intimidate her with his superior size. "Give me back the fucking remote."

She pays no attention to the anger in his voice, shaking her head, enjoying taunting him. "Come tonight?"

"I already I told you I can't." He showers her with saliva as he says this, then sits down again, picking up his phone and ignoring her completely. When the noise starts seconds later, she realises he is streaming the match.

She stands there for a moment, knowing she has lost. "You're so unbelievably selfish," she screams, throwing the remote control at him and marching out of the room.

Later, as she sits at the family dining table with her mother and father, slowly sipping her mother's chicken soup which is just a bit too hot, Lauren dreams up dozens of reasons to stay the night (an appointment in the area the next day, a damaged headlight on her car…) She almost opens her mouth, but then decides against it. Instead, she stays late, later than she usually would, until her mother mentions she is tired and she knows it's her cue to leave. She kisses her parents goodbye, suddenly loving them so much, the tears streaming down her face before she even makes it to her Audi. Her mother waves from the doorstep. It's far too dark for her to see what is happening and Lauren doesn't let herself run back.

Instead, she switches on the engine and takes the long route home, though she doesn't remember making a conscious decision to do so. When she walks into the flat she finds Ryan where she left him, watching some other kind of sport. He doesn't say hello and she doesn't either.

Chapter Two

THE NEXT YEAR

JULIA stands naked in front of her full length mirror. As always, she begins her inspection by turning her body 90 degrees to get the full measure of her double chin, which hasn't receded since she last checked. Then, turning back to face the mirror, she notes her freckles appear larger than usual, while her shoulder length mousy hair is greasy and in need of a wash. Leaning in, she observes her eyebrows are overgrown; she knows she'll have to pluck them later, even though she spent over half an hour on them two days ago. Sighing with despair, she pinches the flesh around her middle and thinks again about the girl in the magazine who sliced off her stomach fat with a kitchen knife. Then she steps in her cramped shower cubicle and beneath the pathetic trickle of water resolves to stop eating altogether.

It's an idea that first came to her in the afternoon, in the wake of a disastrous trip to Selfridges where she had to be wrenched out of a denim dress by a stick-thin shop assistant who scolded her profusely for not choosing a bigger size. Julia had been certain Lauren heard it all, though she never said anything when she emerged from the changing room.

After showering and before going to bed, Julia digs out her holiday clothes from an under-bed storage box, brushing off the layer of dust that has gathered since its last outing. She feels the usual flutter of excitement, knowing the trip is just a day away. It's a trip she never expected to be repeated after Lauren got married. When Lauren called, once again, to insist she book her flights Julia did her best to express her eternal gratitude; were it not for the generosity of Lauren's parents, who would loan the girls their Cannes apartment for a week every summer, Julia would go without holidays.

Now, sitting cross-legged on the colourful rug in her studio flat, Julia uses all the available space to sort her clothes into piles of NOs and MAYBEs, realising nothing in the tired collection she currently owns could qualify as a YES. Among the NO pile are clothes she has kept since the first summer Lauren invited them all to France. None of the sun dresses or strappy tops would fit her now and for a moment Julia wonders why, even back then, she'd been convinced she was overweight. It was the summer after they'd finished school and some of their classmates were going to Ghana to teach orphans, while the rest were attending a never ending succession of music festivals. Julia was invited along to everything, but Lauren made her promise to come to France and she dutifully saved the money from her Saturday job to pay for the flights.

Though she's been away with Lauren many times since, Julia finds herself thinking mostly about that first time, when she walked through the apartment too scared to touch anything because everything seemed precious, even the floor. She remembers so clearly being overwhelmed by the softness of the pillows; she couldn't have imagined a luxury like it and went on and on about it until Lauren snapped, insisting they were just *normal* pillows. The trip was memorable for other reasons too, for the night she and Lauren waited up, not knowing what to do, after Olivia vanished from a club and they were forced to go home without her. At 7am they agreed they should call the police; five minutes later Olivia buzzed the apartment, demanding to come in. There was no apology, just a vague explanation about a yacht and drinking champagne. Then there were five days of Lauren not speaking a word to Olivia.

LAUREN lines up her new bikinis on the bed, feeling more than satisfied with the variety of polka dots, stripes and tasteful frills they offer. Closing her eyes for a moment, she imagines the sun warming her body and lets herself succumb to the illusion of escape. Then she continues packing, with each day accounted for and a couple of options for emergencies.

Later, she shouts to Ryan to ask if he can take her to the airport. He says he doesn't have time and though she knows better than to believe him, she calls an Uber to collect her and Julia; she reasons Olivia lives too far away to come with them and, in any case, she really doesn't want the stress of having to wait around for her. After last year, even Julia suggested they check in separately and meet in the departure lounge.

When the car arrives Lauren summons the day porter to carry her suitcase downstairs. Ryan grunts something at her, but she's in a rush and doesn't go back to find out what he wants. The porter asks if she needs anything doing while she's away and though she can't think of a single job, she confirms to herself he is well worth paying for and that Ryan ought to stop complaining about the service charge for their block.

Once inside the car, Lauren calls ahead to Julia who assures her she is ready and waiting. Moments later she waves them down from the pavement, backpack strapped to her body like a 19 year old about to travel around Nepal. The image instantly troubles Lauren, who remembers, with much discomfort, what happened two years ago, when all three of them were turned away from the port's most talked about nightclub on account of Julia's failure to meet its dress code.

"I know I'm too white," Julia says as she climbs into the car. "I'm allergic to the self-tan. I can't do anything about it."

Lauren laughs, watching her friend strap herself in. "You are looking a bit luminous. We'll have to put you out in the sun."

"Definitely not!" Julia feigns offence and Lauren holds her hands up in defeat, knowing it's not worth pushing. Instead she listens to Julia chat away to the driver like they're old friends; Lauren can tell he likes her as much as they all do.

OLIVIA is chucking most of what she owns in a suitcase when Benji calls to say he's pulled up outside her building. She summons him inside, promising she'll pay for the ticket should he get one, while assuring him he won't; she knows he gets tetchy whenever he borrows his dad's car, even though it's only an old Volkswagen.

Once upstairs Benji stands, jaw agape, in front of the mountain of clothes Olivia has piled inside her case. "You're only going away for a week," he teases.

"It's just easier to pack everything," she snaps, knowing she has neither the time nor inclination to be selective. "Lauren will be taking a bigger suitcase than me and she's got a fully stocked wardrobe in the apartment."

He shakes his head and laughs. "Have you got your toothbrush?"

"Obviously not!" She is stressed now and he seems to sense it, disappearing for a moment and then returning with her toothbrush and toothpaste.

"Thanks," she says, throwing them on top of the mound of clothes. "I just need you to close my case and then we can go."

He groans, but obliges, raising his eyebrows at her lacy lingerie as he removes, neatly folds and repacks everything so it all fits inside the suitcase with ease.

"You should've been in the army," she jokes, reading the satisfaction on his face.

He grins at her, picking up the case and ushering Olivia out her own home. "Your chariot awaits."

"Some chariot," she teases as he holds opens the door to the passenger seat and as always reminds her to put on her seatbelt. She grimaces, but does as she's told, remembering the days when no one cared about seatbelts, when she and her brother would kneel on the back seat of her dad's BMW while pulling faces at the drivers behind. Benji pulls away from the curb and she fiddles with the radio until she finds the station she likes. "Did I tell you Jason is moving back to New York?"

"Which one's Jason?" Benji keeps his eyes on the road, but she sees the hint of a smile creeping across his face and can tell he's winding her up.

"The married one with the bitch wife," she answers anyway, hoping to provoke his disapproval.

"What a terrible shame." He smirks at his own sarcasm and she gives him a playful shove, causing the car to swerve. "Liv!"

"It is a shame, actually," she insists. "You should see him naked."

Benji groans loudly. "I'm sure you can keep in touch."

"Fuck keeping in touch. I'm over it already." She turns up the radio and sings along loudly for the rest of the journey.

Benji stops the car directly outside the terminal building, getting out to retrieve Olivia's bag from the boot and then squeezing her tightly as they say goodbye. "Have a great time and text me when you get there."

"Sure," she agrees, walking off, certain she won't remember.

He yells after her, "Don't worry about me while you're gone. I've got some great Tinder dates lined up."

She laughs, turning round to wave. "I bet you do. Thanks for the lift Benji babes!"

JULIA follows Lauren into the World Shopping store. She yawns involuntarily as her friend debates the merits of two different perfumes with a shop assistant who offers meaningless advice. Julia is unable to help, having been born without a sense of smell, a genetic deficiency inherited from her mother which is mostly annoying, but occasionally has its advantages. When Lauren asks her opinion, her eyes scan the two price tags and she suggests she opt for the more expensive one. "I think you're right Jules," Lauren agrees. "It's more me."

As they're waiting in line at the checkout till Olivia pounces on them from behind. "You made it!" Julia squeals, embracing her friend who is already dressed for the pool.

"Of course!" Olivia laughs, as if it was always a given. She tugs at Julia's arm. "Come with me to buy a magazine."

"Sure." Julia allows herself to be pulled in the direction of the newsagents while looking back apologetically at Lauren who is shouting about meeting at the gate in five minutes. It's been this way since her first day of secondary school, the day she sat down at her designated desk, flanked by Olivia to her left and Lauren to her right. Julia had been worried about being the scholarship girl and the night before had even cried to her mother, claiming she'd never fit in or make friends. She needn't have worried though. Kettle fell perfectly between Johnson and Litchfield in the register and Julia found herself being fought over by the two girls, though to this day she has never worked out why.

Lauren and Olivia were friends already, from the junior school, where they had to sit next to each other for four years on the trot. In so doing, they came to rely upon and annoy each other in equal measure, at least that's how Lauren's mum had explained it to Julia. "They'll always be friends," she said once, when Olivia had called her dad to pick her up mid-way through a sleepover. "Trust me. They'll be over it in a week or so." She was right of course. In the years since, Julia has witnessed many more fights, fights which have barely made a dent in the bond between Lauren and Olivia, their friendship somehow indestructible in spite of its obvious flaws.

"You're like Switzerland," Lauren's mum had said to Julia, on another occasion when Lauren and Olivia had fallen out. "You don't take sides and that's why you're so good for them. You're an old head on young shoulders, far too sensible to get involved in all the squabbles."

LAUREN's bottom begins to numb. She and Julia have been waiting on a metal bench for some time now, watching Olivia argue with an airline representative about her missing bag. Lauren thinks about texting Ryan to let him know she's arrived safely, but quickly decides to message her mother instead. When she looks up from her phone Olivia is standing in front of her, red-faced from shouting. "They'll deliver the bag to the apartment," she announces, "probably today, but I may need to borrow some stuff."

"You always do anyway," Lauren sighs. "Let's get in the taxi queue."

The queue moves quickly and minutes later the three girls have squeezed into the back of a car, with Lauren instructing the driver to take them to Super Cannes in well-practised French. She feels Julia's thigh touching hers and wonders how the largest of the three of them ended up in the middle seat. As a result the journey passes slowly and uncomfortably, with Lauren staring silently out the window for the most part and winding it down intermittently, when the stench of the driver's cologne becomes too much to take. It's only when they reach higher ground that she feels the relief of returning to her second home and the hilltop views her father so often says only money can buy.

Moments later they reach the apartment block with its familiar white walls and opulent display of flora, paid for by its part-time residents; these are mostly English families who bought around the same time as Lauren's parents, when it was the thing to do. Lauren is first to step out of the taxi and she breathes purposefully, allowing the clean air to fill her lungs, a privilege denied to her in London. She pays the driver, tipping generously and leads the way up the wide stone steps into the building.

She sees immediately the apartment hasn't changed. This shouldn't be surprising and yet somehow Lauren expects it to be different, assuming the passage of time would have a greater impact. She slips off her shoes and walks through the large living area towards the balcony, enjoying the cool relief of the marble floors under her feet and studying the view again; the ocean's blue hues are even brighter than she remembers.

"Lauren I need to borrow a bikini," Olivia shouts, already half naked and hopping up and down with the urgency of a hyperactive child.

It's gone midnight when Lauren climbs into bed. She positions herself in the middle of the mattress, enjoying the space. Then she picks up her phone one last time, but puts it down immediately, reminding herself he hasn't called either. She flicks off her bedside lamp, then stares into the darkness while listening to the muffled sounds of Olivia and Julia giggling. She knows soon enough Julia will go to bed, leaving Olivia to watch TV or drink alone on the balcony, depending on her mood.

Lauren wakes early and showers. Olivia has asked many times why she bothers before sun cream and Lauren consistently tells her it just feels better, which is true. She dresses in her bikini and playsuit, then heads for the pool, not yet hungry enough to eat. On her way down she notices the building is quiet, still asleep, and once outside she is surprised to find Olivia passed out on a lounger. She's wearing the bikini she borrowed the day before, in spite of her suitcase now having arrived, making Lauren wonder if she will ever get it back. Claiming the bed next to Olivia, she angles it towards the sun, briefly disturbing her friend, but not succeeding in waking her up.

Lauren slips off her playsuit and lies down, quickly reaching for the latest recommendation from her book club. It's yet another novel set in India, a country none of them have ever visited, but which features prominently in their literary selections. This one feels just like the last and Lauren struggles to summon the enthusiasm for ploughing through more tragedy. Her eyes linger on the same paragraph for too long and she's grateful for the distraction as a noisy group arrives at the pool. Not recognising any of them, she indulges in the joy of wondering who they are and whether they might be worth knowing. Seconds later Olivia groans and Lauren watches her stretch out like a cat coming to from its nap. She sits up, glances down at her body and fiddles with her bikini top. "Shit, I'm getting strap marks!"

"Liv don't," Lauren warns. "There are other people here."

"Oh fuck off Lauren." Olivia unfastens the back and lies down on her front, her modesty only precariously protected. She turns her sun kissed face towards Lauren and whispers, "Who are they anyway?"

"How would I know?" Lauren snaps, wanting to tell Olivia to fuck off herself, but resisting, certain Olivia would actually leave.

"I thought you knew everyone," Olivia yawns, closing her eyes again.

"Well I don't know *them*." Lauren hides behind her book, absorbing snippets of conversation from the other side of the pool; most of what she picks up is about work and property and other people she doesn't know. This strikes her as strange; they sound just like Ryan and his friends, all three of them, with their public school accents and the kind of self-confidence for which parents pay a premium.

"Morning!" Julia drags a vacant lounger underneath the nearest palm tree and Lauren watches as her friend flops herself down, still fully clothed. She feels a twinge of sadness, realising she hasn't seen Julia strip down to a costume in years.

"Hi," Lauren mumbles. Julia smiles at her and removes a small pair of headphones from around her neck, placing them inside her ears. Lauren returns to her book, peeking over the top at regular intervals. She guesses the group must be in their late twenties or early thirties because they don't look too young and they don't look too old. In any case they are quiet now and she can only work with visual clues.

"There's a duck in the pool!" Julia is shrieking with excitement and soon everyone is getting up from their loungers to take a look, united by the absurdity of the moment. Lauren is laughing nervously, but she whispers to Olivia they ought to get it out.

"It's just having a swim," Olivia yawns, holding her bikini in place with one arm. "Don't make a fuss."

She doesn't have to because it's Julia who points out it could poo in the water which is enough to make one of the boys jump in after the bird. He chases it until the duck takes flight and everyone cheers as if he really is a hero, emerging triumphant and somehow even more handsome from the pool.

OLIVIA pours herself a glass of rosé, almost emptying the bottle. The wine had been declared "reassuringly expensive" by Lauren when they bought it from the supermarket a few hours earlier and drinking it now on the balcony, as they watch the sky turn pink, the two girls agree it meets their expectations.

"You know what they say about women with red nails?" Olivia teases, watching Lauren paint each of her toes with meticulous care. Lauren doesn't look up and they sit in silence for some time while Olivia remembers how much fun it used to be, before Ryan, when they were all single and anything could happen.

"I don't think I'll swim again this holiday," Lauren announces, having finally screwed the top back on the nail varnish. "I don't want to catch anything from the water."

"You're more likely to catch something from your husband!" Olivia sniggers, instantly feeling the full force of Lauren's angry glare. She knows Lauren hates being reminded Olivia has been there first, along with the rest of them. "I'm going in to get ready." Olivia senses she has outstayed her welcome and takes the last of the wine inside with her.

JULIA finds Lauren sitting at her dressing table, removing her makeup like she always does before bed. She hovers in the doorway, not wanting to intrude. "There's a problem," she eventually says, when Lauren notices she's there.

She is pressing a piece of cotton wool against one eye and stares blankly at Julia through the other. "What have you done?"

"I've blocked the toilet," Julia confesses. "It's not going down."

She is still hunting for a plunger when Lauren declares she is desperate for the bathroom. Olivia, who has since been informed about the crisis, suggests she wee in the shower, a suggestion that is met with a look of utter disgust from Lauren.

"Why don't we just knock on one of the other flats?" Julia proposes and the others accept it's not the worst idea in the world, even if it's a little embarrassing and perhaps a little late in the evening. They all agree the boys from the pool will almost certainly still be up and almost certainly not mind the intrusion because they seemed friendly enough.

The blonde answers the door. "Help yourselves!" he says, laughing and ushering them in as if he was expecting them, his casual, wavy, hair somehow implying these drop-ins happen all the time. "I'm Dan by the way. The loo's down the corridor. Come have a drink with us when you're done. We've got a bottle open."

LAUREN uses the bathroom first because she can't wait another minute and because she doesn't give the others a chance to get ahead of her. She's instantly relieved to find the toilet is clean and to see the seat has been left down, which never happens in her own home even though she's brought it up with Ryan at least a thousand times.

Afterwards, she waits for Julia and Olivia to take their turns and the girls head back down the corridor together, which is the mirror image of the one in Lauren's parents' apartment except for the modern art on the walls and a different variation of marble flooring.

"Hey, come on in," Dan says warmly and immediately introduces them to Jez, who is reclining awkwardly in a trendy Eames lounge chair, making it look as if he ended up in the apartment by accident and should really have different friends.

"Good to meet you." Jez's voice squeaks like he never quite made it through puberty and Lauren can't help smiling at Olivia because it's the kind of thing they'd have laughed about when they were younger. "Greg's just washing up some wine glasses," he says, gesturing towards the kitchen area. "Oh here he comes.... defender of the pool."

They all laugh and as he walks towards her Lauren senses she is blushing like a teenager. "Hi again," he says, putting down the glasses to shake her hand and then kissing her on both cheeks so she feels the smoothness of his face against hers.

"Is it your place?" Lauren asks later, when they are all drinking wine and the strangeness of the situation they've found themselves in seems to have been forgotten.

"Sadly not. It belongs to my parents," he explains. "They have much better taste than I do."

"They have amazing taste!" Lauren coos, noticing how the room has a distinct, bohemian, personality and how such character is nowhere to be seen in her own parents' apartment.

"My mum's a fashion editor and my dad sells art, so you know..." He tails off and she nods like a student, finding him as interesting as the eclectic mix of furniture. She inhales the soft brown leather of the sofa as he sits beside her, telling her he's been living in New York and she wouldn't have seen him before because there were enough beaches in America for him not to bother with France. She smiles and says she's always wanted to go to the Hamptons. He pulls a face, insisting it's overrated, then says that now he's transferred back to London he plans to take advantage of the Cannes apartment. She doesn't know why this information makes her feel happy, but it does.

"We come every year," Olivia pipes up, reminding Lauren there are other people in the room. "We can definitely show you guys around."

"Sounds amazing," Dan says with a cool enthusiasm, while topping up her wine.

OLIVIA climbs the stairs back to the girls' apartment, avoiding the lift because she has reasoned the noise will disturb Lauren and she could do without her comments. She feels the involuntary sway of her body and clings to the bannister, wondering if she should have let Dan walk her home after all. When she finally makes it to her room she flops onto the bed fully clothed and lets her eyes close. Her head spins and she enjoys the sensation even though she knows she'll be vomiting soon.

The nausea comes on suddenly and Olivia sits bolt upright, trying to make it stop, sober enough to know she shouldn't go to sleep. She takes a gulp from a bottle of water she finds by her bed (she assumes left there by Julia) and breathes slowly, thinking about Benji and how he has so often sat with his arm around her, making her feel safe until either the sensation passes or she vomits into a bowl he has ready and waiting.

She reaches for her phone and punches in his number. It rings, but he doesn't pick up, so she tries again and then again, until she hears his voice croaking hello.

"Hey Benji babes!" she says, the sickness subsiding as she lies back down planning to chat to him.

"You okay? Is everything all right?" he asks, his voice frantic with concern.

"Yeah, everything's good," she whispers. "Just wanted to talk to you."

"But it's five in the morning Liv. I'm asleep." He hangs up before she has time to apologise.

LAUREN is lying in bed when she hears the knocks on her bedroom door. She yells at Julia to come on in, knowing it has to be Julia because Olivia wouldn't bother knocking.

"Sorry to wake you," Julia pokes her head inside the room like a nervous child, "it's just we need to call the plumber and I can't speak French."

"Okay I'm on it," Lauren promises, rolling herself out of bed, while Julia comments on how tired she looks. In her defence, Lauren moans about being woken by Olivia coming home at God knows what hour and they both decide to write her off for the rest of the holiday.

"Dan seems like a nice guy at least," Julia mumbles, following Lauren into the kitchen.

"Yeah I'm sure *he* is nice," Lauren snorts as she rummages through her parents' phonebook, eventually locating the plumber's number.

When she calls, the plumber says he'll be there in under an hour, and Lauren, who is once again desperate for the toilet, is grateful to him when he keeps his word. She opens the door to his bright blue overalls, which hang loosely over a broad pair of shoulders.

"You must be Lauren?" He has a thick French accent, but she is relieved he speaks English. Though his dark skin bears the markings of too much time in the sun, when he smiles there's a softness that makes Lauren feel like she can trust him.

"Thanks for coming." Lauren deliberately keeps her hands plastered to her sides, avoiding having to touch him. "This is Julia," she says, signalling to her friend who steps forward, extending her hand.

"Hi," he says, gently clasping Julia's palm in his own. "I'm Mathis." Julia leads the way to the bathroom, allowing Lauren to hang back and eavesdrop from the corridor. She hears Julia apologise over and over again, and the plumber reassure her he's seen it all before. Julia eventually pops her head out the door to ask for a bucket, which Lauren reluctantly fetches from the kitchen dreading what's to come. She returns to find them laughing and flirting like two people who've hit it off at a bar.

"What did I miss?" Lauren asks, feeling mildly irritated at being excluded.

"Nothing," Julia says, still giggling like a school girl. "He just asked if he could take me out tonight, that's all."

Lauren shoves the bucket into the plumber's hands. "We're busy tonight. Here you go." He ducks back behind the door, recommending both girls remain in the corridor.

"I like him Lauren," Julia whispers, against the soundscape of gurgling and choking coming from inside the bathroom. Before Lauren can respond, the plumber emerges proclaiming success.

"So I will take you out tomorrow then?" he asks, looking expectantly at Julia. She beams back at him, confirming she's free. "Perfect, I will come at eight." He turns to face Lauren. "I left the bucket in the shower. Disinfect it with bleach before you use it again please."

"Don't worry I'll be throwing it out," Lauren says, expressing contempt for the very idea of reusing the soiled item. "How much do I owe you?"

"It's nothing." He smiles broadly, then kisses Julia on both cheeks. "I'll see you tomorrow." Pulling off a single glove, he shakes Lauren's hand and makes his way out of the apartment.

OLIVIA opens her eyes to a sea of yellow and realises she has vomited in the bed. She carefully rolls her body away from it, then covers the evidence with a tissue, resolving to deal with the damage later. She sniffs her hair to check it's vomit free and heads out of the room to look for her friends. Catching a glimpse of herself in the long hallway mirror, she can see she is a shade greener than the night before, though her outfit remains the same. She calls out to her friends. "In here", their voices chime in unison.

"Okay good," she whimpers, sinking to her knees and crawling into the living area. "It's too bright in here." She puts her head down on the floor and stares pleadingly at her friends who pay her no attention.

"There's big news," Lauren says suddenly, eyes lighting up as a wicked grin spreads across her face. "Jules has got herself a date with the plumber."

"What?" Olivia groans. She sees Julia's cheeks flush with embarrassment as she mutters something about the toilet being fixed. "Oh I forgot about that," Olivia admits. She knows she should ask questions, but is unable to form them because she can only think about herself right now. "I feel terrible," she croaks, darting out the room. As she retches into the toilet bowl, all she can hear is Lauren yelling.

"Flush before it blocks!"

JULIA empties the remaining contents of her backpack onto the bed.

"Did you find anything?" Olivia asks, poking her head round the door.

"No it's hopeless," Julia confesses. "I'll have to cancel."

"Don't be stupid! Let me look." Olivia forces Julia out of the way and dives into the pile of rejected clothes. "Hmmm. No. No. No way. Actually maybe. Put this on." She hands Julia a black dress and turns her back. "I'm not looking, don't worry." Julia changes quickly, remembering how she bought the dress in a charity shop and wore it only once to a work event; at the time she received a handful of compliments. Like before, it fits snugly round her chest, then hangs forgivingly over the rest of her body.

"It's on," she says and Olivia turns back around.

"I like it!" Olivia nods approvingly. "You *have* to wear heels though. Have. To." She looks her up and down, making Julia feel uncomfortable. "You need jewellery and a good clutch too. Wait there!"

Julia sits on her bed, feeling her stomach somersault with nerves. "How do you feel about Dan?" she asks when Olivia returns and begins holding an assortment of necklaces and handbags up against her dress.

"I'm in love," Olivia says, her pronounced sarcasm making Julia laugh out loud.

"Glad to hear it." Julia glances at herself in the mirror. "Yes this one could work." She places a chunky silver chain around her neck; it feels expensive.

"It's Lauren's," Olivia whispers. "She won't mind you borrowing it. Just don't ask her."

"Liv!" Julia squeals, quickly removing the chain and handing it back.

"It's fine. She knows. I'm messing with you," Olivia promises, placing a reassuring hand on Julia's shoulder. "Ryan bought it for her. She doesn't even like it."

"That figures." Julia snatches the necklace back. "She barely even mentions him these days."

"What's to say?" Olivia hands her a bag that's definitely too small to hold a snack. "They're married and boring. I'm much more interested in getting you ready for your date." She spins Julia round to face her. "Almost there. We just need Lauren's hair straighteners."

OLIVIA curls her feet up on the sofa and studies the lipstick mark imprinted on her wine glass. Sitting in with Lauren is bringing back memories of forced visits to an old aunt; she would also sigh sporadically in muted disapproval. "Don't you feel like doing something?" Olivia eventually asks and Lauren comments that if Olivia is bored they should knock on at the boys' flat because they'd said to stop by if they were free. Olivia lets out an apathetic, "Nah," and Lauren shrugs, saying it was just a suggestion and she'll do whatever Olivia wants.

"Okay let's go," Olivia relents, springing up.

Greg answers the door this time, his black shirt and smart chinos suggesting he's on his way out. "We're going to that new club at the port," he explains. "You should both come. We've got a table."

"Sounds fun," Lauren agrees, without looking at Olivia.

"Great." His smile broadens. Then he leans over and whispers in Olivia's ear, "Dan will be pleased to see you," causing her heart to instantly sink because there is no thrill in a fait accompli.

"Sorry, just been styling my hair," Dan jokes, stepping into the corridor from his bedroom, his blonde waves as wild as usual. He kisses the girls hello and announces Jez won't be joining them.

"Perfect. It's a double date." Greg holds the door open and the group exit the apartment, Lauren quickly linking arms with Olivia.

OLIVIA is dancing on her own when she feels her heart beat erratically in her head. Everything around her blurs and whirs, while a small, cognitive, corner of her brain demands she get out of the nightclub. She pushes the swarms of half-dressed girls and touchy feely men aside, barely registering their angry protests as she makes for the neon exit sign. A faceless man blocks her before she can get there, swooping her into a cruel embrace, his heavy hand helping itself to her body. She bites and she is released. She lurches towards the heavy double doors. They open too fast and she crashes onto the pavement, where she lies still, waiting for it to hurt.

LAUREN is surrounded by women, all flirting with their eyes and their bodies, some accidentally brushing past Greg, others shamelessly sidling up to him at the table. She can't tell if they are strangers, or people he's met before because Greg dismisses them all quickly, returning to her at once. When she comments she should go home and leave him to have his fun, he laughs and tells her she's being ridiculous because he *is* having fun. Then when she says she's tired, Greg insists on walking her home, which she only objects to momentarily, suggesting she could look for Olivia.

"I'm sure she's busy with Dan," Greg assures her and Lauren takes him at his word.

Outside, the sea breeze blows Lauren's loose hair across her face and she slips her fingers into her handbag, hunting for a band to tie it back. "I look a mess," she says apologetically, when she doesn't find one.

"You really don't." He grins like he's got her all figured out and puts a boyfriend-like arm around her shoulders, which she immediately shakes off, waving her wedding ring in his face. "You are funny Lauren."

"I don't hear that much." She stops short of telling him how often Ryan has accused her of having no sense of humour. They have reached the end of the promenade and they wait at the pedestrian crossing while half a dozen mopeds fly past.

"We'd better get you home before you cheat on your husband," Greg whispers. "I know I'm very hard to resist." She laughs out loud, the tension which has been quietly building dissipating at once.

JULIA is met with silence as she opens the door to the apartment. She finds a half finished bottle of wine by the sofa and she can't tell if her friends are out or already in bed. She'd almost expected them to stay up for her, to want to hear, but she realises it's late now, almost morning. She makes for the kitchen, where she spoons chocolate spread directly into her mouth while waiting for two pieces of bread to brown in the toaster. The sugar hit is instant and her body thanks her a thousand times over.

When it's ready she takes her toast out onto the balcony, watching the sunrise she should have been watching with him as crumbs fall from the corners of her mouth. She plays the night back in her mind: his voice, his touch, him leading her to the beach and her stopping it all so she could go home and eat.

She knows her friends would despair if she told them the truth. Early in the evening she had found the condom Olivia slipped into her bag with a note reading, *Just in case.* It could have gone that way, she thinks. It would have felt right.

They had things in common, things she didn't expect. He grew up listening to the same music, the indie bands she adored, the kind Lauren couldn't bare. He read books. He knew the texts she studied at school and he should have gone to university. He almost did. His father stopped him, insisting he learn a trade, insisting he start earning sooner. He was an only child. Julia understood the pressure and she understood why he left Paris. She often dreamed about leaving London too. "You should move here," he teased.

After a couple of drinks they'd locked tongues seamlessly, but she'd felt self-conscious among the crowds. He realised. He led her to the beach.

"Next time," she promised, when the hunger became too much too bear.

"I hope there is a next time," he said, kissing her one last time and then letting her go.

LAUREN turns the key and slowly pushes open the door, hoping to find the apartment asleep and to slip quietly into her room. Instead she is greeted by the smell of slightly burned toast and she follows its trail to the kitchen, where Julia is loading a plate into the dishwasher.

"Hi," Lauren says softly.

"Lauren! Hi! I thought you were asleep already." A sheepish look creeps across Julia's face. "You caught me snacking."

"So you stayed out late then," Lauren teases, spotting the smattering of wet sand on Julia's legs. "Must have been a good date?"

Julia smiles, her eyes at once dreamy and pathetic. "It was amazing. He's amazing."

Lauren covers her mouth and lets out a lengthy yawn. "Sorry. I'm totally shattered, but I want to hear all about it tomorrow."

"Not much to tell." Julia crinkles her forehead. "Where's Livvy?"

Lauren shrugs. "I think she's with Dan." She blows Julia a kiss. "Night darling. Glad you had fun."

OLIVIA opens her eyes and tries to scream with every part of her being, but there is no sound. Her body is rigid, completely unable to move and yet her mind races with broken memories of pushing through bodies to get out of the nightclub. Feeling the sun warming her paralysed face, she realises it must be morning and that much time has passed.

She has heard about the drugs that do this before and how they slip them in your drinks when you're not looking. There were attacks at her university and although she didn't know the girls personally, their stories were no less terrifying. "Watch your drinks," everyone would say and they did. They were vigilant. They were vigilant for a long time until they forgot and didn't expect it to happen anymore.

The scream rises within her, pushing behind her eyes and through her palpitating heart. Her throat throbs with the pressure, until finally the scream is set free; it flies out her mouth with a force so violent it throws her whole body up in the air. Then she is sitting on a pavement, just a few feet away from half a dozen industrial bins.

She pants heavily, exhausted, but feeling the relief in her shaking limbs as they realise they can move. Standing up slowly, she looks down at her body, her eyes confirming she is fully dressed, though three buttons have fallen open on her top. She can't remember if they were like this before. She can't remember if she had to fight someone off.

Her hands grasp the dark leather handbag hanging over her shoulder. Prising it open she finds everything in place; there is money in her wallet and there are keys to the apartment. She runs, at first only to get away, but later, once she has her bearings, she runs to the apartment, collapsing on the front step.

"Welcome home!" The sound of Dan's voice makes her jump. She turns her head to find him holding open the glass door, a sweatband wrapped around his head. "Sorry. Didn't mean to scare you," he says gently. "Take it you had a good night?" Olivia reaches for the handrail, trying to pull herself up. "You all right

Olivia? You look a bit pale?" He stretches his arm out to help her, but she signals for him to back away.

"I'm fine. It's not what you think," she says, finding her feet and slipping past him into the hallway.

He holds his hands up in surrender. "No need to explain yourself to me. It's none of my business."

"Honestly, I wasn't…," her voice trails off.

He laughs. "I'm off. 10k awaits." He gestures towards the road.

"Good luck," she mumbles, watching him bounce out of the building.

JULIA forces her matted hair into a messy bun, remembering how he played with it, his thick fingers possessing a surprisingly gentle touch. She rubs the sleep from her eyes and leaves her room in search of breakfast, but stops when she finds Olivia in the corridor. "Liv?" Julia says, sensing an otherness to her friend. "I've been worried. Lauren said you left the club with Dan?"

"Sure," Olivia answers, eyes empty like she isn't listening.

"Are you okay?" Julia asks.

Olivia tells her she's fine and that she's going to lie down. Not wanting to leave her, Julia follows her to her room. "Can I make you a cup of tea Livvy?"

"No thanks. I'll see you later." Having said this, Olivia shuts the door in her face and Julia stands there frozen, not sure what she's done wrong. Seconds later she hears Olivia's body crashing onto the bed. Then she heads back to her own room, having lost her appetite.

Once inside she sits there, on her bed, thinking she should say something to Lauren, a thought that instantly evaporates when the phone rings and it's him, asking if he can see her again tonight.

LAUREN stretches out her arm, her fingers frantically hunting for the mobile phone vibrating noisily against the bedside table. When she finds it, she struggles to focus on the screen and it takes a moment for her to realise it's him. "Hi Ryan," she says flatly, closing her eyes again.

"Hi Lauren. How are you?" His voice is warmer than usual, almost rehearsed, like when they first started dating.

"Half asleep," she answers truthfully.

"Sorry. I thought you'd be up." She picks up the sound of the television in the background as he pauses a moment. "I forgot when you're back?"

"Sunday," she yawns. "You know it's always a week."

"Perfect. I'll see you then." He hangs up and she lets go of the phone. It lies beside her on the pillow as she falls asleep again.

OLIVIA punches Benji's number into her phone, having waited until his lunch break to make the call.

He picks up instantly. "Hi Liv. Can you make it quick?"

"Oh it's not important," she lies, not telling him it's taken three days to pluck up the courage to ring him and not telling him how much she needs him to listen.

"I can't pick you up from the airport," he says sharply. "Sorry. I've got a third date."

"I wasn't calling about that," Olivia sighs, upset at being wrongly second guessed, "but that's exciting Benj."

"I have a feeling you'll like her." As he says this his tone softens and Olivia can tell he's smiling. "Call me when you're back."

"Fine." She hangs up.

LAUREN shifts the food round her plate, put off by the bloody appearance of the seared tuna even though she knows it is intentional. She lifts her champagne glass, while Olivia and Julia respond in kind. "Thanks for coming to France with me."

"No thank *you*," Julia interjects, "and your parents too of course!" Lauren notices how Julia has dressed up, how she is letting herself be pretty. She watches her, eating quickly like she's in a rush, and then remembers her saying something about the plumber coming to meet her after dinner.

"What shall we do later?" Lauren directs her question at Olivia, who is staring blankly into the distance.

"I'm going home," Olivia answers flatly, her lips barely moving. "I'm not feeling great."

OLIVIA shudders as Dan's clammy hands land on her shoulder. She looks sanguinely at her half eaten chicken breast wondering if it could somehow save her through food poisoning.

"Thought we'd find you here," he says, crouching down beside her, eyes lingering on her body. "I hope we're still friends."

"Of course," Olivia laughs, wondering what kind of imaginary falling out they've had as she overhears Greg mentioning something to Lauren about their last night. Then all too quickly Julia slips away with Mathis and the rest of them are on their way to a club.

"I think I need to go home," Olivia whispers, letting go of Dan's hand and noticing her palm is already damp with sweat.

"Are you okay?" he asks, eyes brimming with disappointment.

"No I'm not feeling well," she lies. "Carry on without me."

LAUREN sips at her drink, which has been replenished more times than she can count. The hours have passed so effortlessly and when she glances at her watch she is shocked by the time. She thinks about getting up, about leaving, but the bronze lions guarding their table tell her to sit down, to relax. She listens, allowing his legs to brush hers under the table, shifting a little, but letting it happen again and again until her brain catches up with her body and she pushes her mojito away. "I've had enough."

He laughs, moving the glass back towards her. "Don't be boring. I'm having a good time with you Lauren."

"Me too," she smiles, "but it's time to go home."

"It doesn't have to end here," he whispers, leaning in, but still letting her control the moment.

She moves her face away, quickly getting up. "I have to go."

Once she has escaped, Lauren is hounded by competing feelings of longing and shame. She knows she led Greg on, *deliberately* led him on. She's never behaved like this with other men, not even the good looking ones; she's always worried what people would think. Still with Greg she broke her own rules. He made it too easy with his playful banter and his comments that could be read either way. "Your husband is a brave man," he'd said earlier and she'd laughed. "I wouldn't have let you run off to France with your friends."

"My husband doesn't care." She'd let the drink do the talking. She was careless. "He doesn't care at all."

"So he's not brave then," Greg had proclaimed. "He's a fucking idiot."

JULIA rests her head on Mathis's chest as they lie together in a small apartment on the top floor of a noisy block that's not far from the train station. The room is dimly lit by a reading lamp and her eyes dance around finding it all interesting. She didn't expect the space to be full of him, with every picture and piece of furniture so carefully chosen and so completely at ease with its surroundings. Earlier, when she sat on the sofa and he explained it was the only thing he inherited from his grandfather, she immediately felt the comfort of his childhood memories and found herself longing for more of the stories he is only beginning to share. She listens to his heart beating steady and strong, feeling the safest she has ever felt.

"You are beautiful Julia," he whispers. "I don't think you know that, but you are." She says nothing. She can't speak because although it's something her father tells her regularly, she has never truly believed him. Still somehow she feels beautiful with Mathis. Somehow she feels free and in control of the body that has for so long been controlling her. She had been scared of seeming like an amateur and yet, away from the prying eyes of her friends, she became just like them. She became a natural.

Later, when she admitted it was her first time, he said he hadn't noticed. He said he would have been more gentle, but she assured him he was gentle enough. Since then they have been lying together in perfect silence, bar the noise from the street and the neighbours in the block. It's a silence Mathis eventually breaks.

"Don't go Julia. Stay with me here?" His dark eyes promise the things Julia never thought she could have and a lump rises in her throat.

Closing her eyes, she sees her friends' faces when she tells them, hears their arguments and their doubts which are all too easy to predict. There is nothing they can say to change her mind.

"I'll stay."

OLIVIA shuts her suitcase and orders an Uber, quickly scribbling a note for Lauren and depositing it on the kitchen table. She knows there are things she has left behind, but her case is full enough and she trusts Julia to return anything important. Her instinct is to get away and she obeys it, knowing the danger is out there still, a danger she wouldn't recognise if it was staring her in the face.

It's still dark when she gets to the airport, but the passengers are arriving for the early morning flights and the building is coming to life. She catches a glimpse of her reflection in one of the windows and feeling exposed, wraps a cardigan around her shoulders like Lauren would. She is early for her flight; after being told that check-in opens in an hour, she buys herself a coffee and holds it for warmth.

LAUREN finds the door to Olivia's room open. She walks inside, noticing the blinds have been left up as the morning sun shines like a spotlight on Olivia's unmade bed. Lauren makes straight for the window, stepping over the dirty underwear and used tissues left on the floor. She hopes opening it will erase the smell of old vomit which always lingers after Olivia has visited. Resolving to come back later to check, she heads into the kitchen where she piles up dirty plates and fills a bin bag with empty bottles.

The tidying makes her thirsty and she sits down at the kitchen table with a glass of orange juice, spotting the two folded pieces of paper with her name on, which she hadn't noticed before. Recognising Olivia's familiar scrawl, Lauren skims the one line telling her what she already knows: Olivia has left. She scrunches up the note and tosses it in the bin. Then she reaches for the second one, hands shaking.

Lauren,

Don't know what happened last night, but really hope I didn't screw things up.

Have loved getting to know you.

Greg xxx

She makes herself tear it up, hot tears rolling down her cheeks as the tiny pieces fall into the bin, transient as snowflakes. Then she hears the front door open and quickly wipes her eyes.

"Hi Lauren." Julia puts her bag of groceries down on the table. "Did you get the note from Greg? I bumped into him earlier and he asked me to give it to you."

"I did. Thanks Jules." Lauren picks up her glass of juice, still waiting to be drunk, and takes a sip.

"Is Liv still asleep?" Julia asks, emptying the shopping onto the table until it's covered in baguettes and salad ingredients.

"No she's gone. She left a note too." Lauren gestures towards the bin. "It didn't say much."

"Oh." Julia scratches her head. "Do you think she's okay?"

"Who knows? What do you expect from Liv? She always does this." Lauren picks up her sunglasses. "Want to come to the pool?"

"Sure, in a minute." Julia has the nervous twitch of a child who's done something wrong. "I bought lunch for us."

"That's sweet of you Jules. Liv's missing out," Lauren says gently, inching closer to the door. "I'll see you out there."

"Wait!" Julia yells after her. "I need to tell you something."

Later, when Lauren is lying by the pool and the sun is burning through her, she allows herself to cry freely. She cries for a long time, until she is disturbed by the duck returning to the water and performing a victory lap.

Chapter Three

OLIVIA opens the door to her apartment, at once feeling the relief that comes with being in her own forgiving space. She leaves her suitcase by the door and throws herself onto the sofa, fixing her eyes on the large cobwebs that swing from the ceiling like perverse chandeliers. She watches them until her phone buzzes and she gets up to fish it out her bag, thinking it might be him, but finding a message from Julia. She doesn't reply. She lies back down, tears streaming down her cheeks until the cushions are damp and it's dark and there is sleep.

LAUREN does a slow dance around her living room, running her fingers over every surface and caressing every ornament: designer china, Vera Wang photo frames and crystal champagne glasses. Even the dark velvet sofas were bought with donations from family friends and she knows these are her trophies, the hallmarks that set her apart from her unmarried friends.

She stops at her wedding photograph and picks it up, holding it to her chest as she remembers the feeling of accomplishment when she walked down the aisle, even though her corseted dress was bound so tight it hurt.

Then she hears his key in the door and his voice calling her name. She doesn't answer, but soon he has found her and the photograph frame has slipped from her hands, the glass shattering and fragments flying in every direction.

"Jesus!" he cries. "Are you okay? Are you cut?" He rushes towards her and when he reaches her holds her at arm's length, assessing her for damage.

"I'm fine," she says, not feeling any pain as he pulls her towards him in a tight embrace and tells her she gave him a fright. She feels his heart pounding. "Sorry," she whispers, releasing herself from his grip.

"It was an accident. Don't worry." He starts picking up the pieces of glass.

"Leave it," she instructs. "I'll get the dustpan and brush."

She's already walking towards the door when he shouts at her to stop. "You're bleeding!" She looks down to see a trail of blood following her out of the room.

***

Later, Ryan comes to bed earlier than usual, when Lauren is still awake and lying there thinking about their wedding. It had always been an end, she realises, when it should have been a beginning.

"I've missed you Lauren," Ryan says, turning to face her.

"Really?" she asks.

"Really. I know I've been difficult lately. It's just been my new boss stressing me out. Anyway, it's fine now and I'm going to try harder. I promise." It's the first time he has apologised in a long time and as he does so Lauren sees a glimmer of the old Ryan, the Ryan who actually cared.

"Thank you," she says and they fold into each other like they did when they first dated.

JULIA pushes her way past returning stag dos and disorientated tourists, bypassing baggage collection because she didn't bring a suitcase. She promised Mathis she'd be back in a couple of days.

The evening air has a chill to it, a warning winter isn't far away. She's grateful not to be sweating for the first time in months and she notices how it feels easy and effortless to catch a bus to the train station. Once there, she has a 20 minute wait for her train, so she buys herself a chicken sandwich, which she unwraps on the platform, sinking her teeth into the soft British bread and realising what she's been missing.

She has a table to herself on the train - a small victory - and she uses the privacy it affords to flick through her phone, looking at selfies of the two of them and selecting the best ones to share with her parents. She smiles to herself, picturing her mother raising her eyebrows with wonder when she tells her Mathis brings her breakfast in bed every morning. She's prepared for their questions, for all the obvious ones. She expects her dad will brim with pride when she tells him she's at college, learning the language. She knows he of all people would love the beautiful stone building, which makes you feel intelligent before you've even opened a book. In any case, she is certain they'll both be relieved to hear she has made friends and that they'll like the sound of Craig with his Northern sense of humour and Jessica who ran away from an arranged marriage and hasn't looked back since.

There is so much she wants to tell them. So much and so little time that almost as soon as she has arrived she is hugging her mum goodbye and her dad is slipping a £20 note into her hand, telling her to spend it wisely. Her heart breaks again, just as it did when she left Mathis behind. She longs to stay for a couple more hours, but she promised Olivia they'd meet for lunch before she flies and so she goes.

When she arrives at the Hoxton café Olivia is waiting for her, which has never happened before and is strangely unsettling. Julia embraces her friend and feels Olivia's bones poke uncomfortably into her own body. The next hour is spent watching Olivia barely touch the food on her plate and though Julia wishes she knew which question to ask she cannot think of any. Instead she reels off tales of her new life, telling Olivia she's the happiest she's ever been as her friend's eyes betray a sadness she's never seen in them before.

OLIVIA hurls the buzzing alarm clock against the wall, silencing it forever. She pulls the covers, left unwashed for too long, over her face and drifts back to sleep. Benji is in her head again, as always too far away for her to reach him and as always not answering his phone.

Her phone is ringing now, waking her up. She doesn't need to look at the screen to know it's Simon and she lets her voicemail answer, certain he'll leave a message as he loves leaving messages. She lies there for another minute, then rubs the sleep from her eyes and rolls over to reach for her phone, listening to his pompous voice on loud speaker.

"Olivia it's Simon. Can you give me a call as soon as you get this? Your clients arrived an hour ago and I've had to put Camilla on the job. You've lost this one now." As he pauses, she thinks she hears him biting his knuckles like he does whenever he's stressed. "If I don't hear from you by lunch time I'm giving her your other accounts too. I don't know what the hell's going on, but I really hope you sort it out in the next hour, or else you can find yourself another job."

Olivia deletes the message, realising how much Simon reminds her of her father, who is also posh and jolly until you cross him and then there's hell to pay. The smell of coffee wafts in from the neighbouring apartment bringing her back to the moment. She calls Simon and says she's ill.

"Last chance," he warns. "It's your last chance."

LAUREN wanders into the 'head space' zone of her office and sinks into one of the colourful bean bags. She opens the magazine she has picked up from reception and flicks through it without taking in any of the words. No one questions her; this sort of thing is encouraged now and has been since the consultants came in and turned everything upside down. She is grateful for their nonsense today, on her anniversary, when she can't possibly do any real work.

She had woken up happy. Her relationship with Ryan had been getting better and better. She hadn't expected this to happen, but it had. It had happened slowly. They were being nicer to each other, both had made a point of being nicer, or at least more polite, and as each acknowledged the other's niceness it made them nicer still. This morning, Ryan had even presented her with the sapphire earrings she wanted, having picked up on her not so subtle hints. They were back to being good together, or at least good enough and because of this Lauren had woken up happy. Right now though she is not happy.

It was just another Facebook announcement, of which there are at least three a week, but this one affected her more than the others, so much so she put down her sandwich and walked away from her desk. She always assumed she'd be ahead of this girl who only just got married and must have been secretly pregnant at the wedding.

She'll say something tonight. That much she has decided, because Ryan hasn't said anything and she doesn't even know if he's thinking about having a baby, or buying a house, which they should have done months ago. It was months ago when her father told them he'd help with the deposit, which she understood to mean her mother had said something to him, undoubtedly troubled by their tardiness.

JULIA lets herself into Mathis's apartment, panting from the strain of climbing the four flights of stairs. The flat is dark and stuffy, the makeshift curtains having been tightly drawn to keep out the sun. She wipes the sweat from her forehead and runs over to the sink, grabbing a glass from the draining board and filling it with lukewarm water. She gulps it down quickly, finally catching her breath. Then she opens the worn out grey beach bag she takes to the language school each day, removing a couple of heavy books and a large bottle of sunscreen, before eventually finding her phone at the bottom of the bag. His message is there as always, a perfect blend of English and French which makes her smile and wish he could get home from work sooner. Today though, there is also a second envelope, a message from Olivia, which she doesn't need to read to know it's bad news. If anything she's been waiting for it, ever since she saw her, and guilt overwhelms her as her eyes scan the text. *Hi darling, hope you are good? Lost my job today. I'm screwed. Got any good ideas??*

LAUREN parks her car 50 yards away from the house, not ready to drive back to the flat, wanting to stay close. She visualises her offer being accepted, having read about visualisation and how it's supposed to be very effective. In any case she went in over asking price and the agent said he couldn't foresee a problem. She can't foresee one either because she had "the feeling" when she saw it, which was exactly as her mother had described.

This house certainly reminds her of the house she grew up in, being detached and on a good road, two assets deemed essential by her parents, along with off street parking and the potential for a downstairs loo, which of course no family can live without. Lauren can certainly see the potential; she has already explained to Ryan how she'll knock down the internal walls to create a huge kitchen, with an island, and how she'll turn the fifth bedroom into her walk-in wardrobe. He actually seemed impressed with her for once, telling her she had a good imagination and getting excited when she talked about ripping up carpets. Though he moaned about the length of his commute, he called her from his desk less than an hour after the viewing.

Lauren had the foresight to arrange to 'work from home' and she purposefully fires off a couple of emails to give the impression she's being productive. Then eager to stretch her legs, she climbs out of her car, thinking she'll wander to the high street to buy a drink and maybe play at being a local. She doesn't get very far, just a few steps away from her car, when her phone rings and the agent informs her their offer has been accepted.

OLIVIA opens her fridge for the third time, not sure what she expects to find, but still overcome with disappointment when she discovers it's empty. She closes the door and rests her head against it as she plays back her earlier conversation with her landlord, thinking how she could have done without it today and how he's an even bigger asshole than she first thought. Even when she argued she'd never missed a payment until now, not in three years, he'd insisted two weeks was the best he could do and that he was being generous. She'd told him to go to hell.

JULIA sits bolt upright in bed, unable to sleep, tortured by visions of Olivia curling up in doorways. As Mathis snores softly beside her, she runs through the list of people who might offer a solution and even thinks about calling her own parents because they are infinitely kinder than anyone else she knows, bar Mathis, who has already offered to transfer what little money he has to get Olivia a room for a few nights. Reasoning Lauren is in the final stages of renovating her house and most likely still staying with her own mum and dad, she is left with only Benji.

LAUREN closes the cubicle door behind her and unwraps the digital ovulation test. She has a feeling this time, a good feeling about an October baby because she's read being the eldest in the class makes you better at life. When the smiley face looks back at her she instinctively pulls her phone out to take a photograph, before wrapping up and binning the used test strip. Her heart flutters with excitement as she messages Ryan on the way back to her desk. When her phone buzzes almost instantly, she smiles to herself, a smile which fades when she checks the screen and realises it's a reminder instructing her to take a prenatal vitamin.

OLIVIA heads towards his apartment, hauling her suitcase along the pavement. She carries an additional bag of belongings over her shoulder, which is already hurting, but she doesn't have the cash for a cab and she won't ask him for help. She stops a short distance from his front door, still not sure if she's really welcome even though Julia has promised her it will be fine. She looks around, taking in her surroundings like a traveller returning from a long trip. She hasn't dared walk past in months for fear of bumping into him.

As she stands there, the group of youths who have gathered outside the off licence begin talking with raised voices. She knows it could go either way and finds herself walking towards the door, ringing the buzzer just once, not wanting to annoy him. She looks down at the chipped edges of the concrete doorstep and quickly picks up the unmistakeable sound of Benji running down the stairs.

"It's temporary," she stammers as he opens the door. "Thanks for helping me out."

He smiles, not his usual smile, but a steelier one she's only seen him use on strangers. "No worries. Come in. I've set up the sofa bed for you." He takes both her bags and she follows him up the stairs. He stops at the entrance to the living room and steps aside to usher her in. "Make yourself at home." She wants to hug him, but fights the urge even though it's what she would have done before. "Sit down. I'll make tea," he says, leaving her bags in the corner of the room and heading towards the adjoining kitchen.

"Thank you." She sinks into a battered leather armchair, an eBay purchase she warned him about, though it turned out better than expected.

"I hope you don't mind, but my girlfriend is coming over tonight." He is almost shouting over the noise of the kettle and she gets up to be closer to him.

"No of course not. I can't wait to meet her." She hopes her face doesn't betray her disappointment.

"Great. I think you two will really get on." He hands her the tea and then excuses himself, claiming he needs to tidy his room. Olivia returns to her armchair. She sees her everywhere: in cushions with fashionable prints scattered across the sofa and in the scented candles lined up along the window sill. The fire place, previously reserved for Benji's CD collection, is hosting an oversized plant which threatens to sprawl across the whole room. On the ledge above it is a new photo. Wrapped up in Benji's arms, she is prettier than Olivia had imagined, with cute blonde ringlets and innocent blue eyes; she could be a younger version of her father's new wife. Feeling her chest tighten, Olivia wonders why it's so much worse when you can see the attraction.

JULIA vomits into the toilet bowl as Mathis holds back her hair. He tries to persuade her to take a few sips of water in between each round of puking and begs her again to go to the doctor. She cries because she's so exhausted and doesn't want to go anywhere, least of all to a place where she'll undoubtedly be lectured about her weight.

"But it's already booked," he admits, when she tells him she wants to wait another day. "They speak English. It will be okay."

She discards the pyjamas she's been living in for a week and puts on her normal clothes, noticing how they hang more loosely over her body. When she walks into the living room Mathis has taken out the cheese board and the smell sends her dashing back to the bathroom.

Later, she holds the narrow strip of card between her thumb and her forefinger, not sure where she should be looking. "These two lines mean pregnant," the doctor says, pointing to the pink stripes. "They came up right away. I'd say you are quite a few weeks along." He is a tall, skinny, man with an austere face and slightly worn greyish clothes. He doesn't seem like he is joking, but she is sure he can't be serious.

"It's not possible. I'm on the pill," she insists, knowing he is wrong, not allowing the doubt creep in. "There's been a mistake. There has to have been."

He shakes his head, smiling at her through sympathetic eyes. "It's not always 100 per cent effective. Perhaps you had a stomach upset or forgot to take it for a few days?" She remembers now as her palms drip with sweat and the pale brown walls of his surgery seem to pile on top of her. Her mouth fills with saliva. He sees what is happening and shuttles her to the disabled toilet, leaving her to retch in private.

"You're not the first person to do that," he reassures her as she walks back into the room, wiping the corners of her mouth with a tissue. He hands her a glass of water and she sips it gratefully. "You're going to be a mummy. It's good news, not a death sentence." She says nothing. She is worn out, too tired for it all.

He picks up her bag and hands it to her. "I think you should go home, get some rest and let it all sink in. I will book you in for a scan next week so we can find out how far along you are."

LAUREN reads the words over and over again. *Not Pregnant.* This time her body doesn't agree and she resolves not to say anything to Ryan, not until she's sure. She throws away the test stick and determines to test again in the morning, but when she wakes she finds blood in her knickers.

She sits on the edge of the roll top bath and takes a deep breath, accepting the reality and admonishing her body for lying to her. When she crawls back into bed she whispers to her husband, "I've got my period again." He rolls over to face her, still half asleep, then groans softly before starting to snore. She lies there beside him, her mind frantically adjusting the schedule she was working around; she won't be showing off a tiny bump at her cousin's wedding or pulling out of the family trip to Barbados just to be on the safe side.

She feels the tears roll down her cheeks. The GP said to give it a year, but when Ryan wakes up he agrees they should go to a private clinic, to put her mind at rest if nothing else. She calls them immediately and they don't argue, offering an appointment for the afternoon.

Lauren parks her car a block away from the clinic and breathes a sigh of relief when she makes it into the building without seeing anyone she knows. Ryan is already there, in the waiting room, which has been dressed up like the lobby of a luxury hotel, though lacks the cocktail bar and decadent atmosphere. She sits beside him. No one makes eye contact though there are half a dozen women in the room.

Eventually a pregnant assistant walks over to hand them each a clipboard. Lauren fills in the attached forms, wondering if she is giving the wrong answers. Minutes later they're called to the consultation room. The walls are plastered with photographs of babies successfully conceived with the clinic's help and Lauren is sure they are there to taunt her as the doctor recommends a myriad of tests.

She does as she's told. They both do. Then she returns to the clinic alone, telling Ryan not to bother joining and admonishing him for bragging about his perfect sperm count after hearing she needs to discuss *her* results in person. She doesn't need to follow the doctor into the consultation room to know it's bad news; the look of pity on his face is enough of a giveaway. Behind closed doors he tries to reassure her time is on her side and tries to persuade her there are options. He promises her there's still a chance and with the right interventions he wouldn't rule out a pregnancy.

She walks out, knowing she just needs to get to the car. No one stops her and no one asks if she's okay. She climbs inside her black Audi and urgently pulls the door closed, as if it has no windows and actually affords her the privacy she needs. Then she rests her head against the steering wheel and every part of her shaking body succumbs to a pain she has never known before.

Ryan is home early, without warning and she wonders how he knows he is needed. He doesn't flinch when she tells him. He sits beside her at the bottom of the staircase just saying everything will be okay.

"How can you say that?" she yells, jumping up, confronting him and the look of righteous calm on his face. "You don't know that."

He grips her wrists like her mother used to when she was a child. "The doctor didn't tell us to give up. I trust him."

"He wants our money." She shakes him off, pushing past him and running up the stairs, ignoring him even though he is shouting after her, telling her she's being ridiculous. She slams the bedroom door shut and climbs onto her bed, curling her body into a foetal position.

Ryan knocks on the door. "You're phone is ringing," he says, opening it just an inch. "It's Julia."

"I'm not answering. Go away." He leaves the phone vibrating on the floor.

JULIA hangs up, light with relief at hearing Olivia's squeals of excitement. She is hungry again, ravenous now she has stopped vomiting. She hadn't believed the midwife when she said it would get easier in the second trimester, but now she thinks perhaps she might be right.

LAUREN lifts her glass and gently swirls its contents. It's the same breakfast smoothie she has every morning and she forces it down, trying not to taste it and reminding herself a good routine stops the cracks from showing; that's what her mother says in any case. When she's finished the drink, she grabs her phone, punching in Julia's number and waiting for the foreign ring tone. Julia picks up too quickly.

"Is everything okay?" Lauren asks.

"Fine," Julia answers, her voice unusually shrill. "I just have some news. I'm having a baby."

Lauren hangs up, knowing it's all she can do.

OLIVIA buries her head under the pillow, trying to block the noise of her parents arguing, her barely-conscious brain wondering how she can be back there after so long. Finally she remembers. She's not at home and it's not her parents. She climbs out of bed, tip-toes to the wall and expertly places her ear against it. "Please calm down," she hears Benji plead. "She probably thought it was communal shampoo."

"As if!" Bronwyn yells, before the voices become muffled and Olivia is certain they are discussing kicking her out. She climbs back into bed and moments later Benji is shuffling through her room on his way to the kitchen.

"Hi," she says softly and he stops moving. "Everything okay?"

"All fine. Just making coffee." He heads into the kitchen and she follows him, watching him reach for the jar of instant, realising his hands are shaking. "You want one?"

"Sure." She turns on the tap for him and he fills the kettle. They both freeze as they hear the front door slam shut.

"Shit!" He drops the kettle in the sink and water splashes everywhere, soaking the t-shirt Olivia has slept in. "Sorry."

She touches his hand. "Don't be. I'm in the way here."

"You're not," he says gently. "You're not in *my* way." She shoves him out the kitchen, telling him she'll make the coffee today.

Minutes later she finds him lying at the foot of her bed and she waits for him to sit up before handing him his drink. "I'm going to stay with Lauren for a couple of nights," she says, "to give you guys some space."

"Oh so you're speaking again?" he asks, a quizzical expression etched across his face.

"Texting," she laughs. "Julia must have guilt tripped her into forgiving me for the terrible crime of leaving France a day early."

"She probably wants to show off her new house," Benji jokes. "You really don't have to go Liv." He holds the mug against his head as if it might take away the pain of a headache he hasn't mentioned.

She sits beside him, leaning her body against his. "You know what Lauren's like. When she's over it, she's over it. We'll be fine. Anyway, Ryan's away. It's a good time."

JULIA holds the phone to her ear for a long time after the line goes dead, unsure if Lauren heard what she said and unsure if she should ring back. When she does it goes straight to voicemail and she hangs up without leaving a message, happy to see Mathis walk into the room with her pancakes.

As she eats, he sits on the bed beside her, placing a hand on her belly. "The baby is growing."

Julia shakes him off. "No that's just your cooking."

"Uh-uh, it's the baby," he insists, kissing her gently and then getting up again. "I've got to go work." She imagines he is desperate to escape. She wouldn't blame him, not after the last few weeks when she has cried to him every day, relied on him to reassure her, to promise everything will be okay. He didn't ask for a baby either and could easily have sent her home, or gently encouraged her to reach that decision on her own. He didn't. He said nothing made him happier than the idea of raising a child with Julia. So what if it happened sooner than expected? So what? They were grown ups and they would cope. She didn't tell him she felt like a child, barely old enough to have a child of her own in spite of being nearly 30.

"I'll miss you," she whispers.

"Me too." He puts his overalls on and she watches him, feeling guilty. "You can practice your French." He signals to the text book beside her bed and she knows he is right and that she has missed too many classes already.

LAUREN tugs at the drawer beneath her bed until there's enough of an opening for her to slip the leaflets from the clinic between the spare sheets. Satisfied, she walks across the landing to the guest bedroom and plumps the new cushions on the bed, wondering if they look cheap and wishing Ryan had let her spend more. She grabs a handful of cosmetics - all freebies and samples from her skin therapist - and leaves them on the dressing table, assuming Olivia won't think to bring her own.

Then she is done and she waits in her kitchen, staring at the clock on her double oven until the numbers don't mean anything and the doorbell finally rings.

"Nice place," Olivia says, walking in without invitation and quickly kicking off her ballet pumps, which are badly scuffed. Lauren follows her friend into the kitchen, watching her stroke every surface, wishing she wouldn't. "It's so shiny in here."

"It's new." Lauren pulls a stool out from under the kitchen island and Olivia does the same, sitting opposite her.

"I like this. It's very sociable." Olivia helps herself to the grapes Lauren has left out, popping a couple in her mouth. "Crazy news about Jules."

Lauren nods. "I guess so."

"She's happy about it, which is the main thing," Olivia continues, her cheeks still bulging with the fruit.

"Yeah?" Lauren shrugs. "Don't know if I would be. You look like you've lost weight Liv?"

"I'm here to eat," Olivia jokes and taking the cue Lauren slides off her stool and opens the fridge. She pulls out an unopened bottle of white wine, but Olivia shakes her head and for a moment Lauren wonders if she could be pregnant too now, almost expects her to be. She returns the wine to the fridge and fills two glasses with water, setting them down on the kitchen island, along with the assortment of nuts and quinoa crisps she bought from the organic shop.

"I don't think I've seen you since France," Lauren says, passing Olivia the snacks. "I heard about your job. I'm sorry."

Olivia lines up a handful of nuts on the surface in front of her, not once lifting her eyes to look at Lauren. "You could have called."

"And you could have called too," Lauren snaps, finally meeting her gaze, "at least to explain why you left."

"That's true," Olivia admits. She slips off her seat and walks over to the window. "But it's not like you noticed the night I went missing. It's not like you tried to find me at the club or thought to ask where I was when I didn't come home."

"You mean at the port?" Lauren interrupts, trying to catch up. "You were with Dan."

"Not true." Olivia rests her head against the glass. "My drink was spiked. I woke up on the pavement. I'm not entirely sure what happened in between, but I think I fought someone off."

"I wish you'd told me Liv," Lauren says later, when they are pretending to watch a film. "We could've checked the CCTV outside the club and maybe found out what really happened. I mean, I can't bear to think about it and that whoever did it is out there, probably doing it again."

"I was still dressed," Olivia says softly. "I must have got away."

Lauren nods, knowing Olivia needs to believe it, but uncertain whether it's true. "I'm so sorry Liv. I should've realised something was wrong."

Olivia reaches for the folded blanket on the side of the sofa and arranges it over her legs. "Don't be sorry Lauren. I chose not to talk about it."

"I get that," Lauren sighs. "I totally get that." She pauses the film. "Actually there's something you should know about me too. You're probably wondering why I'm not pregnant yet."

OLIVIA lets herself into Benji's apartment. She climbs the stairs and dumps her bag in the corridor before pushing open the living room door.

"Sorry, sorry," she says immediately, backing out the room, wishing she had knocked.

"It's fine Livvy," Benji yells from inside. "Come join us."

She hesitates a moment longer, by which time Bronwyn is forcing her way past her. "I didn't realise you had keys," she says accusingly. "I'm going. I have a big day at work tomorrow."

"Good luck." Olivia watches her run down the stairs, Benji traipsing behind her like a neglected puppy.

"Sorry about that Liv," Benji says, after Bronwyn has gone, his face drained of all colour. Olivia is already halfway through a chocolate bar she's found in the kitchen cupboard and she thrusts it in front of him, offering him a bite. "No I'm sorry Benj. I feel terrible."

He breaks off a slab and eats it quickly, the colour returning to his cheeks. "You did nothing wrong. She shouldn't have been so rude to you. I told her that."

JULIA laughs hysterically as Craig and Jessica fill her in on their weekend road trip to the vineyards. When the story is finished she scans the new emails on her phone. The smile disappears from her face and she walks away from the canteen table, needing air.

From: ll@liebman.com
To: julesk499@gmail.com
Date: 12 March 2015 at 00:27
Subject: Sorry

Hey Jules

I'm sorry we haven't spoken and I'm sorry for writing this in an email, but there's something I need to tell you.

Ryan and I recently found out we may never be able to conceive and right now I am finding it hard to accept anyone is pregnant, least of all one of my closest friends.

I really want to be able to celebrate your pregnancy with you, but I just need a bit of time to come to terms with my own situation.

I hope you understand.

Lauren xxx

Julia places a hand on her stomach, at last recognising the flutter for what it is as a new heaviness takes hold of her heart. She hits the reply button.

From: julesk499@gmail.com
To: ll@liebman.com
Date: 13 March 2015 at 11:42
Subject: re: Sorry

I'm so so sorry Lauren. I love you and I'm here for you.

Julia xxx

It's only when she finishes writing, that Julia realises she has accidentally skipped her class.

"I feel so guilty," she whispers to Mathis as they cling to each other that night.

He lets her go, turning the other way; for the first time she detects anger in his voice. "I told you it's not your fault. Your pregnancy has nothing to do with Lauren. Nothing."

OLIVIA inspects the clothes in her dirty laundry pile, but decides better of it and wanders into the corridor, where she turns the handle on Benji's door. She's alone in the flat, though she still feels nervous as she enters his room. Once inside, she finds his clothes neatly folded in the wardrobe and she picks out a white t-shirt from a pile of half a dozen. Slipping it on she remembers Benji explaining how they fit perfectly under his jumpers and stop the wool from itching. She checks her reflection in his full length mirror, a new addition Bronwyn must have introduced; the outline of her underwear is visible, but Olivia decides her makeshift dress will do until Benji comes home and can teach her how to use the washing machine.

As she leaves the room she spots Bronwyn's make up bag on the floor and her pretty pink night shirt laid out on the bed. She quickly retreats back to her permitted space, where she climbs onto her unmade sofa bed and props herself up with a couple of pillows. She finally opens her laptop, knowing she can't put it off any longer, not after Benji pulled so many strings to get her the work. Minutes later, she feels the adrenaline pumping through her veins just like it used to whenever she was absorbed in a project.

When the daylight begins to fade, Olivia shuts down her laptop accepting she has done enough. The dizziness only hits her when she stands up, reminding her she hasn't eaten all day. She finds a box of unopened crackers in the kitchen and consumes one after another, ignoring the crumbs falling all over the floor. Then she opens the fridge, but closes it seconds later when she spots the bottles resting above it in a small wooden rack. She eyes each one up affectionately, before reaching for a red, a Merlot. After a momentary battle with the cork she pours herself a glass.

When the buzzer sounds it startles her because Benji told her he was working late and never mentioned an Amazon delivery. "Who is it?" she shouts through the letter box, only unlocking the door when she hears Bronwyn's voice.

"I got caught in the rain," Bronwyn says and Olivia realises her blonde ringlets have lost their bounce. "I know Benji's at work.

I'm here to see you." Olivia leads Bronwyn into the living room and offers her a glass of the wine because there is plenty left. "Thanks," Bronwyn says when she hands it to her. "This should help!"

"Just chuck those clothes on the floor," Olivia instructs, signalling to the pile on the tired leather armchair. Bronwyn lays them down gently, while Olivia sits cross-legged on the end of the sofa bed. "So what's up?"

Bronwyn sets her wine glass down on the floor beside her and leans forward in the chair. "I need you to tell me what's going on with you and Benji and I need the truth."

Olivia laughs. "This is going to be a very short conversation. We're friends Bronwyn. That's all we've ever been."

"Bullshit." Though Bronwyn's voice remains calm, her flaring nostrils betray her anger. "You're wearing his t-shirt Olivia. How can you expect me to believe you?"

Olivia looks down at herself. She had forgotten. "I had no clean clothes. He doesn't even know I've borrowed it. I promise you there's nothing going on."

Bronwyn gets up, the floorboards creaking in sorrowful harmony with her heavy steps as she heads out the room. "Things have changed since you've moved in. I'm not imagining it." She stops in the doorway. "I shouldn't have come here."

"Bronwyn he's not cheating on you," Olivia says, jumping off the bed and then chasing her down the stairs. "Honestly. There's nothing between us. Not now, not ever. I'm moving out soon. I've started working again. It won't be long."

"It's too late." Bronwyn opens the front door and shouts over the noise of the rain, which is coming down harder than when she arrived. "We both know he's in love with you." She is gone before Olivia can tell her she's got it all wrong.

LAUREN turns out the lights and crawls under the covers, knowing there's no point waiting up for Ryan because it's always a late night when he's out with clients and he never wants to talk when he gets home. There are a great deal of these nights now and sometimes she wonders if he's deliberately avoiding her. They're not arguing, but there is a new distance between them, a distance that stops them from blaming each other and from saying the things that are better left unsaid. Lying there, she realises she hasn't told him about the party on Saturday. She knows he'll say they have better things to do than battle to talk to people who were once their friends, but are now entirely transfixed on their babies and toddlers. At the last party even Edwin borrowed his niece for the afternoon; they'd mistakenly thought their single gay friend would be the one person they could rely on for adult conversation.

When she wakes Ryan is beside her, sleeping soundly. She watches him for a while, then rests her head on his chest, comforted by the gentle movement as it rises and falls. She begins to drift back to sleep when she feels his hand stroke her hair. "Sorry I was so late again," he says softly.

"It's okay," she whispers. "I know work is busy."

"Listen, I've been doing some research. I want us to see this new doctor I've found. He has a really impressive success rate. I think it's worth a try."

Lauren nods in agreement. "Okay let's see him. I suppose anything is worth a try."

"Only if it's what you want Lauren?" He seems surprised by her lacklustre response.

"It's what's *we* want isn't it Ryan? *We* want a baby." She doesn't even know if this is true anymore, or if she just wants it all to go away.

OLIVIA is woken by the creaking floorboards as Benji creeps past her on his way to the kitchen. "Hey Benj. What time is it?" she asks, rubbing her eyes.

"Sorry Liv. It's 6am. I've got to go in early. Just need to get a glass of water." He whispers even though she is awake and there is no one to keep quiet for.

"It's okay I want to get up early too." Olivia stretches out her body, while her eyes follow Benji's silhouette as it moves towards the kitchen. "I didn't hear you come in last night."

He doesn't answer, so she says it again when he walks back in the room leaving the kitchen door open so there is daylight streaming through. He sits on the edge of her bed, glass of water in hand, and she sees his eyes are bloodshot and that he hasn't waxed his hair like he usually would.

"It was late," he says eventually. "Anyway looks like you had your own party here?"

"What?" she laughs awkwardly.

He signals to the glass of wine Bronwyn left on the floor. "Who was here?"

"No one," she lies; it feels right, like she owes it to Bronwyn. "I was having a drink after my busy working day."

"But there are two glasses." He lifts her own empty glass from the foot of her bed and presents it to her. "Someone was obviously here. It's fine, you can have people round."

"Was just me Benj," she says firmly. "The first glass tasted funny, so I took another one."

"Okay then," Benji concedes, rolling his eyes. "Good luck nursing that hangover. Remember the deadline is Friday." He heads back into the kitchen and she yells after him, telling him it's under control and that he's the only one with a hangover. She hears the tap running for some time before he reappears, looking bemused. "Why was the remote control in the bin? Is it broken?"

"I put it there," Olivia laughs, suddenly remembering. "I didn't want the distraction."

"Right, well, you're a weirdo. I'll see you later." He places the remote back beside the TV as he dashes out the room.

Chapter Four

JULIA forces the maternity jeans past her thighs, but the waistband refuses to stretch over her stomach. She cries as she takes them off, because of the money she wasted and because the effort involved leaves her breathless. Now trouser-less she curls up on the bed, knowing Craig and Jessica, her friends from the language school, won't question her if she says she's too tired or that she has a midwife appointment she'd forgotten about.

In truth she saw the midwife yesterday; she told her to do some gentle exercise, said it would help with giving birth and the recovery afterwards. She didn't say she was fat, but Julia is sure that's what she meant; when Julia told her she could barely walk her eyes widened with shock and she warned her she still has 10 weeks to go. 10 more weeks seem unimaginable to Julia now; she closes her eyes, wondering if she can just sleep through it all because that would make it easier.

The pain wakes her, hitting her suddenly and sharply. She sits up, staggers over to her mobile phone, tears welling up in her eyes as she calls Mathis, barely making sense. She's on the floor when he arrives and she sees the sweat pouring from his body as he tells her the taxi is waiting outside and hurriedly helps her into her pyjama bottoms.

He holds her hand all the way there, saying nothing. When they arrive he leaves her doubled over on the pavement, just for a few seconds, as he runs to find a wheelchair. The smell of disinfectant makes the pain worse and she cries out in agony as Mathis races her through the congested corridors. When they finally reach the maternity ward she clambers onto the floor, unable to sit any longer. They drag her up and make her go to the bathroom before finally letting her lie down in a private room, where an elderly midwife attaches her to machines that beep intermittently. She hears Mathis asks questions, but the woman doesn't answer; she just smears gel over Julia's belly. Then Julia feels something metal and cold pressing down on her skin. "The baby's heartbeat is too slow," the midwife says.

Mathis reaches for Julia's hand again as the midwife disappears. "It will be okay," Julia says. "The baby is kicking me."

The consultant bursts into the room without knocking and without introduction as the midwife cowers behind. Soon he is pressing on Julia belly, moving the metal device around quickly, locating the heartbeat in seconds, a strong and healthy heartbeat. He declares there is nothing wrong with the baby; the midwife picked up Julia's heartbeat by accident. The baby must have been hiding. It happens.

"What about the pain?" Mathis asks. "Is the baby coming?"

The consultant smiles, shaking his head. "Not yet. Your wife has an infection. She needs antibiotics. We'll keep her in overnight." No one mentions they are not actually married.

LAUREN sits at her kitchen island and watches the clock on her double oven as the final hour of her twenties slips mercilessly away. She glances at her packed bag in the hallway; Ryan has told her they're leaving first thing though he hasn't said where they are going. She made it clear she didn't want a party this year and he seemed to understand.

"Let's go to bed," he says insistently, walking into the kitchen. He slips his arms around her waist, resting his chin on her shoulder. "I want us to enjoy the next two days. I don't want you to be tired."

She nods obediently, in that moment realising how frequently she has complained about being tired without explanation, like it's all she knows and nothing to do with blood tests and scans and the horror of being probed like an animal more times than she can count. She slides off the stool and turns to face her husband; there are lines on his face she hasn't noticed before and his eyes have sunk further into their sockets. "I want to stop trying for a baby," she says, surprising herself as if the words escaped before the thought could register.

He says nothing for a moment, but she feels his eyes searching her face. "Really?"

"Really, I mean it." Lauren takes his hands in her own, squeezing them tightly. "I want us to be ourselves again. I want to enjoy life, to go out, to see friends."

"I want us to be happy too Lauren." His voice wavers as he pulls her towards him and she buries her head in his chest, longing to live in the softness of his jumper forever.

"I think we just forgot. I think we forgot how to be happy after this all started. It took everything away."

"We can get it back," he whispers and she thinks he may be crying, but doesn't dare look.

JULIA leans heavily on Mathis as they climb the stairs to their apartment. They rest briefly at every floor and occasionally stop in the middle of a flight so she can catch her breath. She sees his face is racked with guilt and this hurts her more than anything because he has worked every waking hour and she couldn't have expected him to do any more. "We'll move soon," he promises, "as soon as I have the money."

"I'm fine," she says as they reach the top. "I like it here." They turn the corner and she spots the bouquet of red and white roses propped up against the front door. "Did you buy these?"

"No, but I wish I had." Mathis crouches down to pick them up and hands them to Julia.

She buries her bloated face in the flowers. "I can actually smell them. They're beautiful aren't they?"

He frowns, fishing inside the wrapping. "Let's find out who your new boyfriend is." He extracts a note, scanning it quickly as a bemused look spreads across his face. "They're from Lauren."

Julia laughs, remembering. "This is just like the bouquet I held at her wedding. She must have forgiven me." She catches Mathis roll his eyes as he unlocks the door to the apartment, holding it open for Julia who stops suddenly, registering the date. "You know it's Lauren's birthday today. I should have sent her flowers."

OLIVIA is carried out of the lift, moved involuntary along with the swarm of bodies pushing their way towards the trains. She had forgotten the smell, forgotten the dust; as it hits her now she clings to Benji.

"Liv, are you okay?" He pulls her back from the edge of the platform.

"I can't do it," she admits as his body shields her from the throng of commuters. "I want to go home."

"You can do it. I'll take you there. Let's get in the last carriage. It's empty." He guides her and finds them both a seat. "Just breathe. You're ready for this." She nods, knowing the work is not the problem and the money will come easily, too easily. "Go get 'em!" Benji yells as the train doors open and she steps out of the carriage, back into the world.

LAUREN waits for the polish to dry, inspecting her nails and immediately regretting acting on the advice of a 19 year old manicurist. Her legs brush the shopping bags on the floor beneath her and she feels a rush of excitement at the thought of ripping them open and trying everything on again at home. This is her plan for the evening, until she answers her phone and says yes to Olivia. Yes she does want to go out. Yes she does want to celebrate.

The bar is crowded with beautiful people milling around in noisy circles; Lauren works her way around them until she finds Olivia, who has secured a table by the window. There is a glass of Champagne waiting for Lauren.

"Congratulations," Lauren says, hugging her friend, noticing her eyes are sparkling like they used to, before.

"Thanks," Olivia beams at her. "I can't believe it….You look good!"

Lauren performs an exaggerated twirl. "I should do for the amount of money I spent today."

"Good for you. You deserve it." Olivia raises her glass. "To us!"

"To us!" Lauren echoes, lifting her own, remembering a time when this friendship was the biggest and most important thing in both of their lives. For years it was like this. For years they were invincible. "So, you'll be looking for a place I guess?"

"I suppose I should," Olivia sighs, a wistful expression washing over her face.

"Why so sad?" Lauren asks. "I thought you'd be desperate to escape those two love birds?"

Olivia blinks, as if suddenly catching herself. "Oh I am. I can't stand her! It's just the hassle of finding somewhere and," she pauses while fidgeting with a cardboard coaster, "you know, going back to living alone."

"I can understand that." Lauren attempts to disguise the pity in her voice as she thinks about what it really means to go home to someone, even to Ryan. "I'm sure Benji would be happy for you to stay a little longer?"

"I know. I know. He's been totally cool," Olivia agrees, the sadness returning to her eyes, "but I can't. Bronwyn would leave him."

"I wouldn't blame her," Lauren teases, watching Olivia's eyes widen in silent reprimand. "Would it really be such a bad thing for them to break up?"

"Of course it would. I would never do that to Benj!" Olivia snaps. "You know that."

Lauren takes another sip of her drink, realising her glass is almost empty. "We've stopped trying," she explains. "We're having a break from it all."

"Good," Olivia says gently. "I think you need it."

OLIVIA fumbles around for her keys, unaided by the dim glow of the street lamps. "Fuck," she shouts. "This is not what I need." She presses the buzzer, defeated and guilty; a few seconds pass before she hears him running down the stairs.

Benji opens the door urgently, panting a little. "There you are! I was worried."

"Sorry, I lost my keys," Olivia admits, stepping into the hall. "I'll get new ones cut for you. Did I wake you?"

"Wake me?" His brow crumples with confusion. "I've been waiting up for you Liv."

"Why?" She follows his untucked shirt up the stairs.

"Because I didn't know where you were. I called you and texted you and you didn't reply. You know it wouldn't kill you to let me know you'd be late." His scolding tone upsets her and she stops short of following him into the living room. She takes off her coat and hangs it over the bannister, giving herself time to calm down.

"Sorry Benj," she says softly, leaning against the door frame, watching him clear the table of the two settings he has laid. "I didn't check my phone. I didn't realise you'd be worried."

"That's your exact problem Liv. You never think anyone cares about you so you do whatever the hell you like." He stands there, gripping the table, his lips trembling with a rage she's never seen in him before.

"Really Benji?" She marches towards him, leaning in and challenging him from across the table. "I went for a drink with Lauren and I assumed you'd be with Bronwyn. Why are you overreacting?" As she says this she notices the fresh lilies in front of her and next to them, an unopened bottle of prosecco. "What's this?"

"I wanted to celebrate with you." He steps back, throwing his hands up behind his head as his whole body relents and his voice becomes placid. "I rang Mike. He said he gave you both projects so I told Bronwyn I was working late. I assumed you'd be here."

"If you'd have told me I would have come home." She holds his gaze, feeling the shared, unspoken, loss of the evening, while wondering why and wishing she hadn't called Lauren.

"I did call." He walks towards the door. "I'm going to bed."

"I'm sorry," she whispers, wanting to follow him, but remaining rooted to the spot. When she hears his bedroom door close she wanders over to the table and caresses the champagne glasses waiting to be filled, to clink to her success and silently acknowledge how he made it all possible. Her fingers prise open the envelope with her name on it, revealing the simple 'Congratulations' emblazoned on the front of the card. Inside she finds the childlike scrawl she has teased him about so many times before and she holds the card to her chest, playing back her earlier conversation with Lauren. It wouldn't be such a bad thing, she thinks. It wouldn't be such a bad thing to break them up.

JULIA kisses her baby's tiny hands and feet, knowing, with absolute certainty, there could be nothing more delicious. He is beautiful like Mathis, with the same gentle eyes and olive skin, a smattering of jet black hair and chubby arms and legs she just wants to eat. He is perfect and somehow he is everything.

They are waiting for Mathis to return. He promised to bring back treats, agreeing hospital food is a poor reward after everything she's been through. Her phone is buzzing with messages, but she knows they can wait. They will have to wait.

Her child's tiny, crumpled, face looks up at her. "You are a Claude. Your daddy chose the right name," she whispers as his little fingers grip her hand before he falls asleep in her arms. "I can't believe you're here."

The midwife returns to take Julia's blood pressure and to say goodbye because her shift is ending. They met just a few hours ago, when Julia was in the throes of labour, but they hug each other like old friends. "You'll be going home in the morning," the midwife says. "You should sleep now your baby is asleep."

Julia laughs at the suggestion. "I don't want to sleep. I just want to watch him."

"Trust me," the midwife tuts. "You'll regret not listening to me."

OLIVIA flicks through the pile of papers the agent has handed her, feeling him watch her from behind his bright white desk. Sunshine is pouring in from the floor to ceiling windows, triggering a craving for privacy so strong she has to fight the urge to run. She reminds herself Belsize Park is far enough away, far enough not to walk round, not to see him every day. Lauren says she'll like it here and Olivia knows this is her way of saying she may actually visit, a thought she finds unexpectedly comforting as the agent starts talking again. He says, matter-of-factly, that they're the best properties on his books, that she won't find better in the area, not at the price she's willing to pay.

"I'd like to see this one." Olivia points to the only apartment within budget that offers a separate bedroom and living space.

"Good choice!" The agent beams with excitement. "It's just come on the market. I've got the keys. I can take you there now."

"Perfect," Olivia agrees and they walk quickly, the agent spewing out over-rehearsed lines about the merits of the area and name dropping famous faces he's seen drinking in the local pub. They come to a stop outside a grand Victorian building, which he explains would have once been the home of a single family, but is now divided into three flats, all rented by young professionals like Olivia and managed by his agency on behalf of the landlord who lives in Florida. The thought makes her feel a little sick.

"You'll love it here," he promises as he turns the key in the door and directs Olivia up the carpeted staircase to the first floor.

The flat surprises her; its high ceilings and white washed walls create an illusion of space though she knows it's only a fraction of the size of her old warehouse apartment. She drifts happily through the open kitchen and living area into a small double bedroom, with an en-suite shower room and toilet. It feels clean and fresh and empty like a new beginning should. "I'll take it," Olivia says confidently, even though Lauren's voice is loud in her head telling her to think about it and warning her against making an impulsive decision.

"I thought you would," he grins. "Let's sort the paperwork back in my office."

***

Benji's not there. Olivia doesn't know why she expected him to be home, but her heart sinks when she walks into his empty apartment ready to break the news and to see his face fall, ready to let him talk her out of leaving.

She doesn't wait. She begins packing up her things, though she only gets the keys on Monday and has the whole weekend to gather up the few belongings she arrived with months earlier.

LAUREN strokes the screen of her phone, astonished at how Julia's baby looks so familiar even though she's never met him. She feels love and pain flow from her body in equal measure and she bites her lip hard, placing the phone face down on her kitchen island. Though she doesn't want to remember, she still knows where the play mat would go and how the wooden high chair she found in John Lewis would blend in perfectly with the grown up seating around her dining table. Even the empty spot by the sofa speaks of its longing for her old rocking horse, which is still gathering dust in her parents' garage. She dries her wet eyes, letting it pass. Then she goes online to buy Julia's baby a present, spending more than is sensible on an outfit he'll outgrow almost immediately.

"I want to go to France, Ryan," she says when he bursts in through the front door. "I want to visit Julia and the baby."

"Really?" He hangs his coat on the bannister, ignoring the designated space inside the hall cupboard. "Are you sure that's a good idea?"

She reads the worry on his face and immediately resents the vulnerability he's imposed upon her. "I'm 100 per cent sure. We can stay in the apartment. We'll make a holiday of it."

"I guess I could do with a holiday." He yawns and walks towards the kitchen, loosening his tie. "What's for dinner?"

"Whatever you find in the fridge. I'm going to call Julia. I'm sure you'll find something to eat." She turns to climb the stairs.

"I'm ordering pizza," he yells after her.

OLIVIA is woken by the noise of the shutters coming down on the off licence below. She groans loudly, remembering she hadn't meant to fall asleep. She meant to finish packing, but it was harder than she expected to clear her things from Benji's living room; she'd actually felt as if every item was resisting her. Lying awake on top of the sofa bed, the light still on, she remains surrounded by half stuffed bags and piles of unfolded clothes which could be clean or dirty, she isn't sure. The clock on the television informs her it's 11pm. She rubs her eyes and gets up to look for him, already knowing he isn't there.

She picks up the shiny gift bag they gave her in the shop and removes the brown leather wallet, stroking it gently to check it's still perfect. Satisfied, she carefully places it back inside the bag, fishing out the attached card and scribbling a simple "thank you" with the pen Benji keeps in the kitchen. Then she leaves the bag by the living room door and clambers into bed. Her mind restless, she flicks through dozens of television channels, but nothing holds her attention, not like it would when they watch together and seem to find anything on the screen entertaining. Her hands itch to message him, but she resists, knowing she's not his girlfriend and it's none of her business. When infomercials replace actual programmes she switches off the TV and waits for sleep.

She is woken again by the sound of the shutters and she realises the off-licence must be opening for business. She reaches for her phone, but there are no texts, so she calls, hanging on until his recorded voice asks her to leave a message after the tone. Then she types quickly because he has never stayed out all night before and would never stay at Bronwyn's place because her flatmate doesn't approve. *Hey Bronwyn, it's Liv. Are you and Benj okay? I've not heard from him so a bit worried xxx*

She is pacing the room when the phone beeps and when she hears the key turn in the front door and Benji, it must be Benji, stumble up the stairs. She runs out the living room shouting wildly, demanding to know where he's been, her body flooding with relief when she sees him.

"I went out. Is that okay?" He sways back and forth between the walls as he climbs the last few stairs and she picks up the stench of alcohol reeking from his pores.

She spreads out her arms, blocking his path and noticing a stain on his shirt which is almost certainly lipstick. "Why didn't you tell me you broke up with Bronwyn?"

"What do you care?" He pushes past her and staggers into the living room, tripping over an open suitcase. "You didn't you tell me you were leaving," he says accusingly, struggling to get up, the look on his face informing her he already knew. She rushes to help him, but he's on his feet before she gets there and signals for her to back away. "Looks like you're ready to go?"

"I was waiting for you to come home," she says desperately, feeling her heart splintering. "I didn't think Ryan would tell you. I'm sorry. Go to bed and let's talk when you're sober."

"What's the point? You just fuck off when you're ready." He limps out the room and seconds later she hears him crash onto his bed.

"When did you become such an asshole?" she yells into the wall that separates them. Then she finishes packing and takes an Uber to Lauren's house, grabbing the shiny gift bag on her way out.

JULIA steps back from the Moses basket, listening to him snoring, confident the baby is really asleep this time and praying she'll have an hour to herself as she quietly confronts the full length mirror she's been hiding from for months. Once again she studies herself from a multitude of angles. Her fleshy stomach, now partially hollow and hanging low over her pubic bone, shows no sign of shrinking back to what it used to be pre-pregnancy. Though the midwife told her the weight falls off with breastfeeding, she realises now it's another myth, merely part of the propaganda to keep babies off the bottle.

Disgusted with her body, she opens the broken wardrobe she shares with Mathis. Her old clothes remain shoved into a corner and while she longs to wear them, ordinary as they are, she knows better than to try any on. She knows better than to abandon the maternity leggings and shapeless t-shirts that have been her uniform since Claude was born. She even reasons it's better and somehow less upsetting for Lauren to see her like this, so utterly broken by motherhood.

Hearing Claude stir, she rushes towards him and gently rocks the basket, hoping, in vain, to settle him. She looks at the clock, its long hand taunting her. He didn't even give her 15 minutes and he is done, the endless hours of the afternoon now stretching ahead like an impossible endurance challenge. Mathis already warned her he'd be home late; though he did a good job of looking heartbroken when he kissed her goodbye, she almost told him she hated him. She almost told her mother she hated her too, when she called her, like she does every morning, just to see how Julia is doing. She wanted to scream at her for not visiting, even though she knows she can't afford the air fare because the boiler blew up and their savings went on its replacement. Mathis's parents have let her down too, visiting only once when Claude was three weeks old and proving themselves to be too old and too ill to help.

Claude is crying now, screaming. She picks him up, rocks him and soothes him with her shushes realising there can be no respite from her new role. When the crying eventually stops – it must be at least 45 minutes later - the silence is beautiful. She strokes his tiny face and there is a first smile, the first effort he has made to show her he loves her. "Thank you," she whispers, smothering her baby in kisses.

Chapter Five

OLIVIA walks slowly to the coffee shop, enjoying the fresh air and the compelling spectacle of designer prams and dog walkers who are out in their droves. They have started to recognise her in the shop now and she looks forward to the three minutes of chat about the weather or what she got up to at the weekend, as well as the way they try to tempt her with a muffin or a piece of cake, knowing she'll politely refuse, joking she's watching her weight. This one trip out of the apartment each day is enough for her and the days go by quickly, the hours devoured by impending deadlines and the kick she gets from beating them, from delivering better work than they expected and immediately being asked to do more.

She collects her coffee and heads to one of the empty tables, brushing away the crumbs left by an earlier customer. In her mind, she rehearses what she's going to say to Lauren, a half-truth about work being too busy and Julia promising to visit soon in any case. She knew instantly she didn't want to, physically couldn't, go back to France, but she pretended she'd think about it and promised to get back to Lauren with her decision.

Her phone rings and she blocks another call from Benji. He calls every day around this sort of time and she never picks up, not even now he has stopped leaving messages and she is starting to forget the sound of his voice. The dentist waves at her from his booth in the corner of the shop. He is also here every day, taking a break from the clients who pay a small fortune to be seen at his surgery next door. They met in the queue, just a week after she moved to Belsize Park, when she sniggered at his order of a herbal tea and he informed her coffee would stain his teeth, which are perfectly white, but not blindingly so. She waves back and he strides over to chat, asking her out again, while she laughs as always, not quite saying yes and not quite saying no. He isn't fazed by her uncertainty, perhaps, she thinks, because he's older. She guesses he's approaching 40; he can't be far off, not with that much grey hair. He wears it well, along with the stubble and the thick framed glasses that define his face. She enjoys flirting with him, but it's enough for now.

LAUREN searches her handbag again, checking every pocket, every place she might have packed them. The Mediterranean sun beats down on her dark hair, making her feel too hot and making it all too hard.

"I've left them in London. I must have done. They're not in my bag," she announces to her husband, giving up.

"Look again Lauren. You definitely have them." He snarls at her like an angry dog and drops the suitcases. "You need to find the fucking keys now."

"I'm telling you I've left them behind." She doesn't stop him from grabbing the bag and turning it upside down. "Oh," she says, picking up the keys and handing them to her husband. He battles with the lock on the heavy glass door, while she gathers her belongings from the front step.

"Thank God," she mutters as she hears the door open and follows her husband and suitcases into the communal hallway, not noticing the door being held open for them.

"Cheers mate," Ryan says casually and she looks up, realising Greg is saying her name, saying it more than once because she isn't responding.

"You two know each other?" Ryan asks and her mind searches for answers because she can't pretend they haven't met.

"Yes, sorry, this is Greg," she stutters. "Hello, hello. I'm so sorry, I was in a daze. Too much sun already!" She pats down her cotton dress which has become crumpled, then looks up at Greg's amused face, which bears no hint of embarrassment.

Ryan extends his arm. "Great to meet you. I'm Ryan," he pauses, inflating his chest like a puff adder, "Lauren's husband."

"I thought as much," Greg says smiling, shaking his hand. "My parents own an apartment here. I met Lauren and her friends when they were in town last summer."

She feels Ryan place his hand on her shoulder. "Lauren you're really red. Are you okay?"

"I need some water. I'm too hot. I'd better go up." She snatches the keys from Ryan's hands and rushes towards the lifts, her heart pounding heavily as her flushed face threatens to give too much away. "Good to see you again," she mumbles as the elevator doors close, leaving behind a scene she has no control over and which she can only hope plays out in her favour.

Upstairs, Lauren pours herself a glass of water and paces the living room in heated, but silent, conversation with herself. The facts soon speak for themselves, reminding her she resisted and declaring her innocent in her own moral court. She is disturbed by Ryan banging on the door, which she opens for him and the suitcases. Then she slinks over to the sofa.

"He seems like a nice enough guy," Ryan gasps, still breathless from carrying the bags.

"I guess so. I don't really know him." Lauren closes her eyes, hoping to end the conversation.

"I said I'd play golf with him." Ryan flops down beside her, stinking of BO. She wants to tell him he needs a shower, but the exhaustion has become real and she hasn't the energy. He places the back of his sweaty hand against her forehead. "You okay? You're still very red."

"I just need to rest," she says, swatting him away.

OLIVIA feels the grease cling to her finger tips as she runs her hands through her unwashed hair. She picks her black leather trousers off the floor, then spots an emerald green blouse lying dormant on her velvet armchair. She sniffs it briefly, allaying her concerns, and dresses quickly. Dashing into the bathroom she swirls a mint flavoured mouthwash round her gums, spits four times into the sink, then heads out the flat, acquiring a pair of eight inch heels and a trilby hat en route to the door.

She walks faster than usual, shooting past the coffee shop, pretending not to look in and pretending not to see the dentist pretending he isn't waiting for her. She's not late, but she rushes to the underground, just wanting to be there, to get started, knowing this is *her* event and she has to pull it off without a hitch. She insisted on the hotel in Soho. She insisted they send out the right message with the right kind of pastries and fancy coffees.

When she arrives she sees immediately she was right about it all and she watches her guests fall for it, convinced beyond doubt by the glamour of the chandeliers and unnecessarily sparkly furniture. She watches them, every snotty journalist and self-important representative from the biggest retailers, as they come to the same realisation: they need her client's product, a £300 beauty device, to matter in the world.

She checks his name is still on the guest list and as the compliments fly in Olivia's direction she looks for Benji everywhere, expecting a tap on the shoulder at any minute. Soon enough there are goody bags and thank yous and there is plenty of clearing up to do. The client sees her collecting plates from a table and tells her to leave it. He insists on buying her dinner, pointing out she's been on her feet all day and hasn't eaten a morsel. She tries to say she is busy and needs to be on her way, but he won't take no for an answer. He says he is not that kind of man and she should know that. She smiles. She's seen what happens when he walks in a room, how he has an unmissable presence, not because he is tall and broad and not because his nose is far too big for his face. Beyond his bushy eyebrows lies an unshakeable confidence in himself, a confidence which makes everyone around him fall into line.

Olivia follows him out the hotel, her heart sinking when she spots the rest of his team sloping off. They get a table easily and he orders the wine, which is more than reassuringly expensive. When she attempts to steer the conversation back to business, his eyes glaze over. He wants to talk about her he says, to get to know her better. He's intrigued. His hands creep across the table and she recoils, not meaning to knock over the wine and then rushing to save what's left in the bottle. He accepts her apology, grabbing her napkin and insisting it's just a splash, nothing to worry about.

As they eat their main courses he talks at her, telling her about the boat and the chef and all the things that would have impressed her once upon a time. She pretends to listen, wishing she'd soaked him through, enough to end their evening and to avoid being presented with the dessert menu. She says she has a headache, probably from the long day and when he accepts this excuse she lets him pay the bill without putting up a fight because he's still the client. He helps her into her coat and says he wants to take her home. She says, "No," politely at first, then less so when he objects, walking quickly, managing to scramble herself inside a black taxi and instruct the driver to go and not to let him in as he tries to pull open the door. She hears the familiar clink of the lock, as the taxi screeches away from the curb.

"You okay love?" the driver asks.

"Fine now. Thank you. Belsize Park please." She twists her body until it hurts and she has a clear view out the back window.

"We've lost him love. He won't be able to follow us in this fog. Don't worry."

LAUREN climbs the dusty stairwell to Julia's apartment, taking care not to breathe too deeply nor allow any part of her body to touch the sweaty walls.

She finds the right flat and, seeing there is no bell, she knocks on the door, immediately worrying she's woken the baby. Julia shouts from inside, "Come in, it's open," so she pushes the door slowly, popping her head round first, afraid to intrude. She finds Julia on the floor, crouching over the baby. "Sorry about the smell," she says, holding two tiny legs in the air. "Just changing a nappy. Won't be a minute."

"No problem," Lauren laughs, keeping to the other side of the room and finding an ancient looking sofa to perch on. She looks around, absorbing the brownness and realising the walls and windows are ingrained with what must be decades of dirt. She thinks back to her childhood and how her mother redecorated their house every three years, which she used to find tiresome, but now understands completely; this is what happens when homes are neglected and when people can't afford to pay for a cleaner. In the middle of the bubbled linoleum floor she spots a pile of nappies and other baby-related gear she can't quite identify, but which at least lend some colour to the room.

"I can't believe you're here. I'm so happy." Julia flashes Lauren a grateful smile as she clambers onto her knees, her baggy t-shirt barely disguising the belly fat protruding over the top of her leggings. She lifts up the baby, now fully clothed in a stained sleepsuit, and delivers him to Lauren. "This is Claude," Julia says, her voice full of a pride. "Want to hold him while I wash my hands?" She doesn't wait for an answer and forces the baby into Lauren's arms.

Lauren cradles him as best she can, though he is wrigglier than she had expected and it takes her a moment to realise he is twisting his neck round to look at her. She alters her position, allowing him to study her face. "Hello Claude," she says softly. "I'm your Aunty Lauren."

"I think he likes you," Julia teases as she walks back into the room. "If you're lucky you'll get a smile." Lauren accepts the challenge and pulls a series of silly faces, the kind she's seen her friends pull often, the ones who have babies. She's relieved when Claude gurgles approvingly.

Julia is down on the floor now, moving things around and making piles, but not really tidying. "Sorry it's a bit cramped in here. We only have the one bedroom, so all the baby stuff is in here."

"It's cosy," Lauren says, trying to be polite, imagining it's what Julia would say if the situation was reversed. "In any case it's bigger than your London flat. Mind you, that was a shoe box." Claude smiles, her chat apparently entertaining him. She looks over at Julia. "I can't believe I'm holding your baby."

"I can't believe I have a baby," Julia laughs, getting up off the floor and sitting beside her on the sofa. She offers her hand to Claude, who grips her little finger. "He'll fall asleep soon I expect. You okay there or should I take him?"

"I'm great," Lauren admits, stroking his tiny face as she pulls him a little closer so that he rests his head against her chest and she feels the warmth of his body and the rhythm of his steady breathing. "He's so small."

Julia nods. "I know he's just a little thing, but believe me he's taken over my life. It's like I'm suddenly living in a parallel universe where my days revolve around feeding him and burping him and changing him. There's literally no time for anything else. It's relentless. Sorry, I don't mean to complain."

"Don't worry," Lauren says gently. "You really don't have to watch what you say around me. I'm okay."

"You seem to be," Julia whispers, her eyes misting over. "It's just not fair though is it? It happened to me when I wasn't trying and it's all you want."

"Don't think like that!" Lauren interrupts. "I'm happy for you. I truly am. Claude is amazing and I love him." She scrunches up her nose and passes the baby to Julia. "You can take him back though. I think he's just been to the toilet again."

"This is what I mean," Julia laughs, lifting him up and sniffing his bottom. "It never bloody ends." She carries the baby back over to the sponge change mat and begins to undress him. "Anyway Lauren, how are things with you?"

"They're fine. No news." Lauren straightens out her top which has become creased from holding the baby. "Greg's back in town. You know, from the flat below."

"Oh really?" Julia looks up. "That's cool."

"It was strange to see him again actually. It all got a bit intense last year. I mean, I think he wanted more." Lauren wills Julia to understand as she watches her pinch her nose in anticipation of removing Claude's nappy.

"He knew you were married, right? You didn't *do* anything?" Julia asks, eyes suddenly wild with indignation as she leaves her half-dressed baby to fend for himself on the floor while she bags up the nappy and leaves it outside the front door.

"Of course I didn't do anything," Lauren cries after her. "It was just weird to see him and now obviously Ryan wants to play golf with him, which I could definitely do without."

Julia returns to her child, saying nothing as she buttons up his sleepsuit and gently places him in his Moses basket. She picks it up and begins to swing it back and forth between her legs. "Trying to make him sleep," she explains, now swinging the basket more vigorously. "I wouldn't worry about Greg. Sounds like there are no hard feelings on his part. I can't see him causing any trouble." She lowers the basket to the floor and crouches down beside him, catching her breath. "He's almost off. I'll leave him a minute."

Lauren kneels next to her, watching the baby drift in and out of consciousness. "I said some things to Greg," she whispers, "about stuff not being great with Ryan. I mean it was nothing, just a rough patch, the newlywed blues I guess.

"Are things okay with Ryan now?" Julia asks, her mouth creasing with concern.

"They're fine now. Thanks Jules. Like I said it was the newlywed blues and well Greg was there and for a minute or two I might have thought the grass was greener, that's all."

"I guess it's different for me," Julia says softly, standing up and stretching out her limbs. "Men fall in love with you all the time, but with me it's just Mathis. No one else has shown an interest, so there's zero temptation. There's definitely no other grass."

"That's ridiculous," Lauren snaps, in hushed rebuke, conscious of the baby who is now fast asleep. "Of course other men could fall in love with you. Everyone loves you."

Julia laughs. "I doubt that, but it's kind of you to say so Lauren. Look I'm simply pointing out it's easier for me because men don't notice me like they notice you."

"Trust me Jules, I have a hard time getting my husband to notice me." As she says this Lauren realises just how little her friend understands and resolves to say no more on the matter, instead presenting Julia with the present for Claude, for which she expresses far more gratitude than is necessary. After this moment of lightness, the conversation runs dry and Lauren makes an excuse about needing to get home for an early dinner with Ryan. As she hugs Julia goodbye, Claude wakes up, letting out a scream so piercing it breaks Lauren's heart.

"He's hungry," Julia explains, rushing to pick him up. "This child is always hungry. He won't stop screaming until I feed him. Sorry!" She scuttles to the sofa and fumbles around inside her top. "I hate these maternity bras. They're so tricky to undo."

"You do what you have to do," Lauren shouts over the noise. "It was great to see you." She closes the door behind her, running down the stairs and straight into her Uber, which is already there by the time she reaches the pavement.

JULIA closes her eyes as the baby feeds, trying to ignore the tugging on her breast and the feeling she's slowly dehydrating. She realises she's forgotten to fill her plastic bottle with water and decides she can't get up now; she is certain Claude will be inconsolable if she tries. As he sucks, her mind runs through all the things she needs to do before she can hope to go to bed. She wonders if she could skip his bath, just this once, without it messing up the routine he is finally beginning to respect, and she considers leaving the dirty nappies for Mathis to take out. She can't imagine mustering the energy, not today, not after Lauren.

It's been dark for some time when she hears his key in the door and she doesn't get up from the sofa because Claude is asleep on her shoulder. She should have put him down in his Moses basket – she could have claimed 20 minutes for herself - but she chose to hold him, remembering her mother telling her, in a recent phone call, to cling onto these moments while they last, because they are finite in number and gone too quickly.

"How was it?" Mathis whispers, kissing both mother and child.

"Hard," Julia answers, not knowing how else to describe it and feeling a sadness overwhelm her at this admission of failure.

"I'm so sorry. Sometimes friends do grow apart. " He reaches for Claude and carefully transfers him to his own shoulder, barely causing the baby to stir. "You go sleep. You look tired."

"Thank you." She obeys even though she longs to spend time with him, creeping next door, lying down on top of the covers and instantly falling into a deep sleep.

OLIVIA slams the door of the Uber as she jumps out into the traffic. The Euston Road isn't moving and she knows it'll be quicker if she runs, especially since she had the foresight to wear trainers. When she arrives, she dashes through the hospital's automatic doors, barely aware of the tears streaming down her face as she begs everyone she encounters to tell her where they've taken him. A Filipino nurse with a sympathetic demeanour eventually takes pity on her, walking her to the ward, where she speaks to another nurse who has the look of someone who is permanently harassed and tells her he's in surgery already and she can't see him yet. She instructs Olivia to wait in the corridor, where there's a seat for her and a view of the city she'll be able to see when the fog clears.

"He told me to call you," the second nurse says. "I'm the one who left the messages."

"Thank you." Olivia recognises her voice now, the slight Cockney accent, the matter of fact tone. "I'm so sorry. I hadn't charged my phone."

"It happens," the nurse says gently, sitting down beside her and putting a chubby arm around her shoulder. "You're here now."

"I'm too late," Olivia whimpers. "He must think I hate him."

"I doubt that very much. Don't give up on him yet. He's got the best team of doctors in there. There's a very good chance he'll pull through." The nurse hands her a tissue. "Dry your tears. That's right. Now breathe."

Minutes later Benji's parents appear, eyes empty as if the world has forsaken them. His dad gives Olivia a hug, while his mum just smiles through her tears, explaining they'd popped out to get some air because they didn't know what else they could do. They look older and greyer than Olivia remembers; this is all she can think about as they talk, filling in the gaps before Olivia has a chance to ask. They came as soon as they heard about the crash, his mother says. They were there when he was awake and still completely lucid, reassuring them not to worry. They thought he'd just broken his wrist, maybe cracked a rib. It was only later when they discovered he'd pierced his spleen, when they heard the words "internal bleeding" and a dozen doctors came running from out of nowhere. Olivia stops listening because the details don't matter.

A third nurse shakes her awake. "Morning pet. He's come through surgery. He's asking for you." She has a big smile plastered across her face. "He's a bit groggy, but he's doing well. You can go in for five minutes. His mum and dad have seen him already and have gone home to get his things. Don't tire him out now."

"I won't. Thank you," Olivia croaks, her dry throat making it hard to speak. Picking herself up, she takes a few steps towards the curtain and pulls it back.

"Hello stranger," Benji says, his voice weak, but warm and familiar, reassuring Olivia the swollen, cut, face looking back at her is really him.

"Looks like you've got yourself in a real mess." Olivia sits on the chair beside his bed, wondering how many others have sat in the exact same spot feeling the same mix of fear and gratitude she feels right now. Resting her head on his mattress she turns her face towards his.

"They told me you've been here all night," he says breathlessly.

"I hope you appreciate the effort?" She squeezes his plaster free hand and he nods, immediately wincing with pain. "Take it easy Benj," she whispers and he waits, though the intense, pained, look in his eyes lets her know he has more to say.

"I was on my way to your event," he eventually gasps. "I wanted to support you. How did it go?"

"It was fine," she says, remembering, knowing she couldn't possibly tell him the truth, not now. "I didn't realise..."

"I've missed you Liv," he cuts in. "You know I'm sorry."

"Shush," she whispers. "It doesn't matter. You don't have to talk. I'm just happy to be here."

Seconds later the nurse pulls back the curtain. "You need to rest Benjamin. Your girlfriend can come back later."

LAUREN splashes her face with cold water and pats it dry, feeling the momentary tightness in her skin that occurs before she applies her moisturiser. She moves quietly through the apartment, not wanting to wake Ryan and knowing, if left undisturbed, he could easily sleep until noon and she could have the morning by the pool.

When she gets outside she's struck by the intensity of the heat, a warning the rest of day could be unbearable and certainly hotter than usual for the time of year. Casting aside her floral sarong she squeezes her sun lotion into her palm, carefully covering her whole body and finally massaging the cream into her concave stomach. The sadness takes her by surprise, like it so often does, and she wills the thoughts to go away, opening her book and escaping into someone else's tragedy.

She remains in this other world until she sees a shadow creep across the page and looks up to find Greg standing at the foot of her lounger. "Didn't mean to startle you," he says and she notices the beginnings of a pot belly resting above his long, navy, swimming trunks.

"You didn't." She sits up, reaching for her sarong and wrapping it back round her body.

Greg parks himself on the lounger beside her. "It was good to meet the famous Ryan." As Lauren feels her cheeks flush red again, she sees the teasing grin spread across his face. "Relax! We're fine. I'm happy you worked things out."

"Thank you," Lauren mutters, not quite relieved, a small part of her wishing he'd made it harder. "Are your friends coming out here too?"

"No, I'm on my own. Needed some space, a rest. Things have been so hectic with work. I need to get healthy again. I mean look at the state of me!" He points at his rounded stomach, making Lauren laugh until she catches the wounded look on his face. "Thanks a lot. You're supposed to tell me I look great."

"Ummm," she says, unable to wipe the smile from her face.

"Well you look great. Ryan is a lucky man." He gives her a playful wink. "I'll tell him when I play golf with him tomorrow."

"Don't you dare!" She pretends to whack him with the corner of her sarong and he jumps off his lounger.

"Right, well I'm going to swim 50 lengths while you just sit here looking pretty." He immediately leaps into the pool, deliberately soaking Lauren.

"You're not funny," she yells, watching his head pop up from under the water.

"I'm hilarious." He runs his fingers through his wet hair. "You should join me. There are no ducks today!"

"No thank you." Lauren returns to her book, thinking about her conversation with Julia and the grass which, in truth, probably isn't any greener and yet somehow appears lusher than ever before.

JULIA feels the sweat patches forming on her t-shirt as she weaves her way through the cars and tourists to her lunch date with Lauren. She left late because it was hard to leave and even now she is worrying about Claude. He was still crying when she closed the door, but Mathis insisted she trust him and promised her the baby would be fine. It was his idea for her to see Lauren one more time, away from the apartment and away from the baby. He wouldn't let her cancel, wouldn't let her use Claude as an excuse and insisted it would be too rude to let her down last minute.

Lauren is already there, waving at her from a table in the middle of the narrow restaurant, one of many on the Boulevard de la Croisette Julia deliberately avoids. As she makes her way towards her friend, she notices the space is full of people who look like Lauren with their expensive clothes and designer sunglasses that are too big for their botoxed faces. She almost trips over a small dog, which is poking its head out of its owner's handbag.

"I'm sorry," Julia pants, clutching the back of her designated chair.

"Don't be silly. You have a baby," Lauren says mercifully, standing up to embrace her. "I'm starving. Let's order." She beckons for a waiter to come over and he signals he'll be there in a minute.

"Oh, I might just have a drink," Julia says quickly. "I'm not so hungry."

"Lunch is on me," Lauren interjects, reading her mind and shoving the menu in front of Julia. Julia scans the sheet of paper, freshly printed with the day's specials and prices that make her eyes water. "You must eat something. I want to treat you!" Lauren says, her tone resolute. "I insist. No arguments."

"Thank you. I suppose I could manage a bowl of pasta," Julia concedes, putting the menu down. Lauren laughs, suggesting she order something more French. "No I'm sick of French food!" Julia says defiantly, as the conspicuously French and overfed waiter arrives at their table. Julia orders her pasta and Lauren requests a Salade Niçoise, a dish, Julia notes, she frequently eats in London.

When the waiter retreats, Lauren leans across the table. "Ryan is playing golf with Greg right now," she whispers.

"Are you worried?" Julia mouths back.

"Yes. No. I mean I think we're okay." Lauren's face suddenly lights up. "I saw him by the pool and he said he was happy for me. It just makes me feel a bit weird, the idea of them hanging out together."

The waiter returns with their drinks and the conversation stalls until he is gone, at which point Julia tells Lauren she's sure it will be fine. They sip their Diet Cokes in silence. "Did you hear about Benji?" Julia asks at last.

"Yes!" Lauren gasps. "Ryan got a text from his friend. I meant to call Olivia actually. I forgot. I must do that."

"She messaged me," Julia confesses. "She's been at the hospital for the last two days. It's been pretty full on I think."

Lauren raises her eyebrows. "Wow. That's intense for Liv. Perhaps she's finally realised she can't live without him?"

"Lauren!" Julia cries, even though she's been thinking the same thing.

Their food arrives and Julia has to stop herself from eating too quickly; she usually only manages a few mouthfuls before she's forced to abandon her plate. It feels like a luxury now, to finish a meal while it's still warm, and she does this while listening to Lauren chat away about everything Julia isn't missing about London. Other than Olivia, she never warmed to Lauren's circle of friends, finding them mostly dull and universally unpleasant.

Once her plate is clear, Julia feels the unwelcome heaviness return to her breasts and she lets Lauren know it's time to go home. There is a flicker of sadness in her friend's face, but she summons the bill and hands her bank card to the waiter. He returns moments later with the card machine and hands it to

Lauren for her pin, deliberately looking in the opposite direction as she punches in the number.

"I'm sorry," the waiter says in English, once the machine is back in his possession and Lauren is applying a fresh coat of lip gloss, "your card has been rejected."

"Are you sure?" Lauren asks brusquely, giving Julia a knowing look, the kind she understands to mean she's dealing with an idiot. "Can you please try again?"

The waiter obliges, though Julia notices him tutting quietly to himself. When the same thing happens again, Julia offers to pay, taking cash out of her purse that was meant for nappies.

"It's fine, I have another card," Lauren snaps. "This is my treat. Something must be wrong with the machine." The waiter gives Julia a knowing look, as Lauren hands over an alternative. This time it works, allowing Julia to put her money away. She thanks Lauren for her generosity and rushes off, conscious of the breastmilk leaking into the pads she's stuck inside her bra. Instinct tells her Claude is starving and hysterical, but when she gets home she finds him asleep in his father's arms.

LAUREN sits on the sofa, touching up her nail polish and wondering, with increasing anxiety, what is taking so long.

"I need a shower," Ryan shouts, bursting into the flat and heading straight for the bathroom. She lingers on the sofa for a few more minutes and then heads to their bedroom, where she unfolds and refolds her silk negligee, until steam fills the apartment.

"Why do you make the shower so hot?" she asks Ryan as he walks into the room. "You're ruining my hair." He doesn't answer. With a towel wrapped round his waist, he poses in front of the mirrored wardrobe and runs a hand through his thick brown hair. Lauren pulls a face. "How was the golf?"

"Yeah, good," he says, turning to look at her. "He's not a bad player. We had a burger afterwards."

"Oh great. I'm glad you had fun." She watches her husband remove the towel from around his waist and rub his upper body dry. It's a routine Lauren's witnessed countless times; next he'll put on his boxer shorts and spray his whole body with deodorant, an act she's often declared excessive and for which she blames TV advertising. After that he'll retrieve a pair of pale chinos from the pile inside his suitcase and ask Lauren where she's put the T-shirts he left on the floor. She'll roll her eyes and point him towards the wardrobe. This sequence plays out exactly as she expects, reminding her how well she knows her husband.

"How was lunch?" Ryan asks, when he is sitting on the bed next to her and putting on his socks.

"It was really lovely," Lauren answers honestly, "much easier than last time." She watches Ryan get up, reach for his wallet and slip it into his back pocket. Then she remembers. "Our bank card didn't work. I had to use the emergency Visa my dad gave me. It was really embarrassing."

Ryan furrows his brow. "That's weird. I'll call the bank and get it sorted. Don't use it for the next week or so."

"Oh, okay," she agrees. "I'll just have to reimburse my dad when it's fixed." She notices Ryan's towel lying on the floor and she picks it up. "You know there's a thing called a peg!"

"Sorry," he mutters and walks out the room.

"Where are you going?" she shouts after him, but he doesn't respond. She knows her mother would call it selective hearing, but Lauren is certain he's just being rude.

OLIVIA dashes to the bathroom. Though she has tried to leave her flat three times already she hasn't made it past the front door. After flushing the toilet she faces herself in the mirror above the sink. "No more!" she commands and though the nerves are incomparable to anything she has ever felt, she makes it out the building and onto the underground.

"You're going to be carrying the bags for once," Benji jokes, while Olivia surveys the cubicle, checking he hasn't left anything behind. For the first time she notices the paint peeling off the walls and the sheer ugliness of the space Benji has occupied for weeks. "Let's get out of here," he says, draping his arm round Olivia and relying on her to keep him steady as they make their way outside into the warm embrace of the sunshine. "I just want to feel it on my face," Benji says, stopping for a moment. "I've missed it."

Olivia watches him, eyes brimming with the tears she has hidden from him until now.

"Come here." Benji pulls her in towards him. "I'm still alive Livvy, although if I don't kiss you now I might actually die." His warm lips press against hers and she picks up the mint residue of his toothpaste, realising he has prepared for this moment, the thought of which amuses her greatly.

Inside the car Benji shifts awkwardly in his seat. "It won't be much longer," Olivia promises, squeezing his hand and willing the London traffic to disappear. In the silence that follows she thinks about the earlier kiss and how it can only mean this is it and she is his. The sadness ripples through her body as she concedes the loss of her single life and the possibilities it offered.

"Thank you," Benji says softly.

"For what?" Olivia asks, troubled by the earnest expression on his face.

"You know, for being here." He looks away self-consciously.

"It's fine. I had nothing better to do today. Don't go getting all soppy on me Benj." She digs her nails firmly into his palm.

"Ouch!" he yelps. "I forgot how evil you are."

***

The day runs away into the inevitable night and the dread creeps up on Olivia like a stalker. She stalls before she climbs into the bed because Benji is there already. Though they've slept under the same covers hundreds of times before, neither one of them can pretend it isn't different now. Minutes earlier, Benji had offered to sleep on the sofa and they'd both laughed, agreeing *that* would be ridiculous. Olivia made the point that if anyone should sleep on the sofa it should be her because she isn't injured, but Benji insisted that would be ridiculous too.

Now, as Olivia slowly pulls back the covers, she feels him looking at her in the way men do. She lies down, wishing she'd worn more than the small vest and pyjama shorts that cover only the parts of her he's never seen. In the next moment she is up again, pulling down the blinds and blocking the light seeping in from the street.

"Liv," Benji whispers as she climbs back into bed, "you know I want you more than anything?" She says nothing as she feels her body seizing up. "My ribs are broken though, so I'm afraid I'm not up to much."

"That's too bad," she teases, the power returning to her limbs and allowing her to find him. "Go to sleep," she whispers, kissing him softly and then rolling back to her side of the bed. She reaches for his hand, which he gives readily, and they sleep side by side, as if this is how it's always been.

Chapter Six

LAUREN lines up the organic ingredients on her kitchen work top and tosses them, one at a time, into the blender. She watches as the banana, kale and berries lose their identity to the destructive blades of the whirring machine. When it finishes, she hears Ryan slam the front door behind him. Then she pours the contents of the blender into a tall glass, which she carries over to the kitchen island. Sitting down, she drinks quickly before the taste can hit her palate, rewarding herself with a women's magazine. As she flicks through, she circles the products and styles she's keen to try, which isn't many on this occasion. When she's done, she heads upstairs, picking Ryan's dirty clothes off the floor and wiping away the facial hair he's left in the bathroom sink. Afterwards, she applies her makeup, experimenting with a lighter shade of lipstick she deems appropriate for the summer months. She completes her outfit with a navy, fitted jacket, which she'd laid out, ready and waiting, on the bed.

Once downstairs, Lauren collects her handbag from beside the front door. She notices the post lying on the mat and picks it up, speculating whether there's a new postman doing the rounds because it doesn't usually arrive before she leaves the house. Flicking through the pile, she finds a red bill, a final warning which sends a shiver down her spine. She stares at it in disbelief, remembering, with absolute clarity, Ryan setting up the Direct Debits to pay the bills automatically so she wouldn't have to worry.

With the letter open before her, she sits at the bottom of her staircase and punches Ryan's number into her phone. She seethes with frustration as it goes straight to voicemail and decides, given the urgency of the matter, to try him at the office.

"Good morning, Ridgemont Finance. How can I help?" The receptionist delivers this greeting with great speed, making it a challenge for Lauren to decipher its meaning.

"Can you put me through to Ryan Liebman please?" Lauren eventually asks and is instantly put on hold. Soft rock music blares down the line while she waits for what feels like too long. Then the music stops abruptly.

"I can't find a Ryan Liebman," the receptionist says, her tone now weary and unfriendly. "Are you sure he works here?"

"Of course I'm sure. He's my husband," Lauren declares, determining to complain to Ryan about the women's incompetence and attitude, which certainly aren't in keeping with the prestigious reputation of the firm. "Can you at least put me through to Accounts?"

"Putting you through now," she sighs and the music starts playing again.

"Hello Accounts, Justin speaking." His warm, Irish, voice puts Lauren instantly at ease.

"Hi Justin, it's Lauren Liebman. How are you?" she asks, remembering how much she likes him.

"Lauren, what a surprise!" he roars with such volume she pictures him announcing her to the entire office.

"Oh, I'm just trying to get hold of my husband," she explains. "The receptionist couldn't put me through for some reason." Lauren thinks she hears Justin muffle the phone with his hand. "Justin, hello?"

"Sorry. I'm right here," he answers. "This is a bit awkward, but Ryan doesn't work here anymore Lauren. He left two months ago. I'm really sorry. I thought he would have told you."

"Right, of course." She tries to stop her voice from shaking. "Sorry, I forgot he'd moved. I'm an idiot. Sorry to bother you Justin."

"No problem at all. You have a good day now," he says and the line goes dead.

Lauren's phone flies out her hand as she clutches her chest, fearing it might explode. When the sensation eventually subsides she sits at the bottom of the stairs with her head between her knees, breathing rapidly. There must have been a mistake; this is what she thought, at first when her card was rejected, then again when the red bill landed on her doorstep, and once more when the receptionist at Ridgemount Finance told her she couldn't find Ryan's name on the system. Now she sees there is no mistake and she dashes to the downstairs toilet, expelling the vomit she's been holding in her mouth as Justin's words ring in her ears.

A little later Lauren arrives at her office, slipping in unnoticed as her colleagues absorb themselves in tea making rituals. Switching on her computer she retrieves the bill from her handbag, reading it one last time before paying online using her father's credit card. She reasons her dad won't pay the card off for a few weeks yet, which is enough time, she hopes, to figure out an explanation.

Later, when the afternoon draws to a close, she pops her head round the boss's door and asks if she can take the following day off work. He nods to signal his approval, which she had anticipated given his heavy reliance on her father's business.

Lauren arrives home before her husband, as is normally the case and as usual, she empties the dishwasher before preparing dinner. She assumes Ryan will be eating with her because he hasn't said otherwise and she seasons the chicken and vegetables the way he likes them. Then after texting her mother a photograph of her efforts, knowing she'll be proud, Lauren puts the tray in the oven and watches it cook until she hears Ryan's key in the door.

"How was your day?" she shouts out to him.

"Long," he groans wandering into the kitchen, his skin bearing the familiar grey tint it acquires at the end of the day, "just the usual dramas."

"I've made us dinner. Come sit down," she instructs, quickly laying their usual places at the kitchen island, one opposite the other. She watches him wash his hands at the kitchen sink and dry them on the towel she leaves beside it, a habit she's taught him.

"Smells good." He kisses her on the forehead and slides onto his stool. "I'm starving."

"Good," she says and they eat together as man and wife, with Lauren commenting the bins need taking out and that they ought to buy a get well gift for Benji, which Ryan insists he doesn't need because he's not a woman. After consuming everything on his plate, Ryan leaves it on the table and walks out of the room, proclaiming himself exhausted. As Lauren clears the table, she hears the television come on in the lounge and after loading the dishwasher, claims the space beside Ryan on the sofa. She rests her head on his shoulder, picking up the distinctive scent of the shampoo he imports from America for its anti-hair loss properties. He's always taken his hair seriously and she doesn't blame him for this; he's kept his looks far longer than the majority of her friend's husbands.

"You okay?" he asks, perhaps because she is quieter than usual.

"Fine," she answers and they watch the television together in silence, before Lauren heads up to bed, assuming he'll follow in an hour or so because he usually does.

JULIA opens her eyes to the morning light, which is seeping through the gap beneath the curtains. She is up like a shot, rushing to the foot of the bed where she finds Claude in his Moses basket, breathing softly, his cheeks reassuringly pink. Her breasts ache with fullness and she immediately worries her baby is hungry. She shakes Mathis until he groans. "He's still asleep," she whispers. "It's 6am."

"Is he okay?" Mathis asks, peering at Julia through half-closed eyes.

She nods. "I think so. I just can't believe he's slept so long."

"It had to happen one day. Claude is three months old now. Go back to sleep." Mathis pulls the covers over his face, letting Julia know he is done talking. She lies beside him, eyes wide open, waiting for the cry; it comes soon enough, along with the relief of feeding him. She strokes Claude's soft hair, praising him for being such a good boy and imagining a time when the fog of exhaustion might finally lift, a fog so dense it has blinded her to the possibility until now. Claude pulls away from her breast and gazes up at her. "I love you too," she says, "even more today than yesterday."

LAUREN reaches for her phone to check the time; no light passes through her black out blinds and she has been waiting, for what feels like hours, for 6.50am, when Ryan's alarm clock will reliably go off as it has done every weekday for as long as they've shared a bed. She sighs, discovering it's still only 6.24am, knowing there is no hope of falling back to sleep as her mind runs through all the possible excuses and explanations that would make everything okay. Over and again she pictures him attending one job interview after another, planning to tell her everything when he has good news to report, at which point she forgives him, saying she understands.

When the alarm sounds she lies still, listening as the gentle music quickly transforms into an unbearable drone, finally prompting Ryan to turn it off. As he does so, Lauren turns to face away from him and his bedside lamp, which he flicks on, illuminating the room. The bed rocks like a boat as he climbs out; seconds later she hears the clunk of the hot water tank, signalling he's jumped in the shower. Lauren would normally drift back to sleep before Ryan returns to the room, but she remains awake and focussed on her plan. Once he's out of the bathroom, Ryan fumbles around the closet for a work suit, making plenty of noise. Lauren stretches convincingly, then slopes out of bed to find the tie he thinks he has lost. Then she showers, as she usually would.

Afterwards, she finds Ryan in the kitchen, drinking his first black coffee of the day. As always she tells him he should eat something, knowing her advice will be ignored. Then she assembles the ingredients for her smoothie and watches him walk out, while announcing he'll see her after work.

She waits for him to close the front door, then opens the hall cupboard to retrieve the dark hooded top she purposefully left there, pulling it over her fitted work dress and leaving the house. She carries an envelope in her hand, ready to post in case he should see her, but he doesn't and she follows him to the underground station, lifting her hood up over her hair.

The train is waiting and Lauren has to run to make it, jumping through the closing doors while ignoring the warning to steer clear. The carriage isn't crowded and she positions herself by the window at the end. It affords her a view into the adjacent carriage where Ryan has taken a seat in the middle of a row and is staring, with some interest, at the adverts opposite him. At each new station the train gets busier, eventually obscuring Lauren's view of Ryan and forcing her to push her way towards the main doors. From here, she sticks her head out at each new stop, hoping to spot him getting off. Though an ugly man in an expensive suit suggests she move further down the carriage, she refuses to budge, paying no attention to his dirty looks or those of the other passengers. When the train pulls into Euston, where Ryan would normally get off, she sees no sign of him and she remains in her carriage. Just one stop later, at King Cross, she finally sees him scamper across the platform.

She moves quickly, fearing she is too close and then hanging back, momentarily losing him after he steps off the escalator. She looks frantically in every direction, eventually spotting his thick brown hair heading into a tunnel. She follows him, the sound of a saxophonist's mournful melody echoing within the tunnel's walls as Ryan leads her to the westward branch of the Circle Line. She hides behind a family of Chinese tourists, watching him pull out his phone, check something and put it straight back into his pocket. A gust of filthy air signals the train's imminent arrival and Ryan steps forward, slipping quickly inside after the doors open and the departing passengers have exited the carriage. Like before, Lauren stations herself in the next coach, more confident this time round, the thrill of the chase very nearly superseding her profound sense of dread. As each stop approaches she prepares to move, but Ryan is nowhere to be seen until they reach Edgware Road station, when he races past her carriage. She catches him up, remaining just a few feet behind. One after the other they exit the station and take a left turn onto the main road, where they keep pace with the crawling traffic until Ryan eventually crosses the street. Lauren watches him from the other side, remembering him promising never to touch cocaine again and swearing the night with Olivia was the very last time.

Ryan stalls outside a large Argos, checking his phone and then quickly turning the corner, where he heads through a side entrance. Above it Lauren reads the sign for the Grosvenor Victoria Casino.

***

The house is still when she returns. The ingredients for her smoothie remain untouched on the kitchen island and she gathers them up, chucking them in the bin to make space for her laptop. Hands shaking, she waits for the computer to come to life, then immediately logs into her online banking account, a joint account set up when she and Ryan first married and into which both of their salaries are supposedly paid. She's never checked; she has always left the bills to Ryan and spent as she sees fit on the debit card attached to the account. Now, as she scans the online statement for the first time, she sees the negative numbers running into the thousands, her latest pay cheque instantly withdrawn and nothing coming in from Ryan. The vomit works its way up to her mouth and she dashes to the kitchen sink.

In her heart she already knows it's gone and running up the stairs she almost wonders if she shouldn't check, if she could possibly pretend a little longer that it's all still there. She doesn't stop though and opens the drawer, finding the velvet covered jewellery box inside. She prises it open and sees it's all missing: her grandmother's diamond necklace, the Gucci bracelet from her parents and even the sapphire earrings he bought for their first anniversary. Staring at the empty box, she remembers, so clearly now, her aunt arriving at the house. She'd never seen an adult cry before and Lauren ran to hug her before being immediately ushered upstairs and told to play in her room. After dinner she overheard her parents talking using words she hadn't heard before, but were definitely bad, to describe her uncle. "I can't believe he took the school fees," her mother would say, over and again. Years later, when they were looking at old family photos and Lauren asked why her aunt and uncle had divorced, her mother simply said, "Gambling," and looked sad like she would if a relative had died of Cancer.

Lauren closes the jewellery box, placing it back in the drawer where she found it. Then she heads downstairs, fetching the step ladder from a cupboard in the kitchen and dragging it up to the first floor landing. It gives her just enough height to open the hatch to the loft, which is not yet fully converted and used mostly for storing suitcases and other things, mostly Ryan's, for which there is no obvious place elsewhere in the house. She pulls down the ladder attached to the hatch and scales it quickly, finding the two old suitcases she's looking for and throwing them down, creating a cloud of dust in the process. She waits for it to settle, then climbs down. In the bedroom, she flings open the doors to the shared walk-in wardrobe and gathers rail after rail of Ryan's clothes, paying no attention to whether she is creasing his shirts or crumpling his trousers. Then she raids the bathroom for every single one of his cosmetics and doesn't stop until everything is shoved into a suitcase, ready to leave. It all happens without a morsel of food entering her mouth, without a single tear being shed and with only a brief moment of reflection, where Lauren wonders, just for a second, if she'd be doing the same thing if she was pregnant with his child.

Later, Lauren waits on the doorstep with the suitcases, not knowing what time Ryan will be home, but trusting he'll be back. It's a warm enough evening, but that doesn't stop her from shaking and she zips up her hooded top; there was no time to change after she spent an hour with the locksmith and another hour on the phone to the bank, freezing Ryan's access to the joint account.

She sees him at last. He's walking quickly from either excitement or agitation, she can't tell, but when he spots her he stops dead, resting his hand on the front gate. "What's going on?" he asks. "Are you okay?"

"I know," she says, blocking the entrance to her home as she watches him make his way cautiously up the drive.

"What are you talking about?" He furrows his brow, feigning concern for and reaching out to touch her. "Lauren, are you okay?"

She shoves him hard. "Don't come anywhere near me. You're moving out."

He shakes his head, reaching for her again as she retreats further into the doorway. "I don't understand," he says. "What's the matter?"

"Don't pretend Ryan. I already told you I know." She speaks calmly, her words decided in advance and practised to perfection. "You have lied to me, you have stolen from me, you are gambling away everything we own and I want you out my life." In the light emanating from the house she watches every muscle in her husband's face contort with pain, a horror she has only seen once before when he got the call about his father's first heart attack. He puts his head in his hands and hides there for a long time.

"I can explain," he says at last, uncovering his face and revealing eyes that are red and desperate. "It's not what you think and I'm going to get it all back I promise. I just needed some cash. It's all going to be sorted soon."

He reaches out for her again, but she side-steps him, pushing the suitcases towards him. "That's not how it works Ryan. You could have come to me. You could have told me you were in trouble. My dad would have helped you. You absolutely know that."

"Lauren, you have to listen to me. I'm going to sort this out. I've got cash on me now. Look!" His temples appear to pop out of his forehead as he pulls a stash of notes from his back pocket. "I've got what I need. I can walk away."

She hears herself saying, "No," as she places his hands in hers, the money crumpling in her palm. "One win at the casino won't solve our problems. It won't make up for the lies you've told me.

It won't make up for anything." She steps back, wiping the tears from her face, tears she hasn't been aware of until now. "I think you should go to your parents."

"I'm so sorry Lauren. I've fucked up, I know." He sobs loudly, at once more child than man.

"It's not enough to be sorry," she says coldly, though it pains her to see him looking so pathetic. "You need to leave. Shall I call your dad or do you want to do it?"

"I'll do it." He walks to the other end of the driveway and makes a call, which ends quickly. "My brother is coming," he says afterwards and she nods approvingly.

They wait there, not saying anything to each other, until the navy BMW pulls up outside the house. Ryan rolls the suitcases towards the car, signalling for his brother to pop open the boot and then loading them inside. For a moment Lauren thinks he's going without saying goodbye, but then he heads back towards the house, to where she is standing on the doorstep. "I wanted to give you everything," he says softly, "I honestly did."

She hugs herself, aware of a sudden fear, perhaps loneliness. "Well maybe I asked for too much."

"You didn't." He leans in to kiss her cheek and she doesn't object. She waits until he is really gone, until the car has driven away and she can't see or hear it anymore before she unlocks the front door with her new set of keys and steps back inside her house.

OLIVIA overfills the tea cup, not noticing as the boiling water dribbles slowly towards her fingers. "Ouch," she cries, when she finally feels the burn.

"You okay?" Lauren yells from the sofa.

"Fine." Olivia dashes to the sink, shoving her hand under the cold tap. "This is why I never make tea," she jokes as Lauren gets up to collect her own drink. They sit down together, Olivia taking the sofa and Lauren the old leather armchair; it was a condition of Benji moving in that he could bring the chair with him and Olivia didn't object.

Olivia gestures to the tin of shortbread on the coffee table. "Benji bought them. Help yourself."

"Thanks, I'm okay. I've lost my appetite a little," Lauren says, holding her mug close to her chest.

"Sure you don't want to share?" Olivia opens the tin, taking one for herself.

Lauren smiles, shaking her head. "I feel like a fucking idiot."

"Don't!" Olivia cries, wiping the biscuit crumbs from her mouth. "You've not done anything wrong. No-one saw this coming."

"I'm keeping the house." Lauren continues, as if having the conversation with herself. "I know it's got memories, but I love it. I chose everything in there and I want to stay. My dad's going to buy out Ryan's half." She raises her eyes to the ceiling. "I still believe it's going to be my family home one day."

"It will be," Olivia agrees, her heart swelling with sadness for Lauren and also for the loss of her own family home; sometimes she goes there and sits on the bench outside, needing to be close, imagining her parents, rather than strangers, are still inside. "You're young and you're beautiful and you'll meet someone in no time," she says to Lauren, wanting to be kind.

"The last thing I want is to meet someone," Lauren snorts and Olivia considers herself silenced. She longs to tell Lauren there are better men than Ryan, men like Benji and men like Mathis, men who are good right through to their core, but she doesn't say anything. Instead, she takes another bite of her biscuit, realising, in a rare moment of self-castigation, she is failing miserably in her role as a friend. This thought is confirmed when Lauren stands up, announcing she has to leave.

"Really?" Olivia asks. "I'm not up to much today. You can stay as long as you like."

"Thanks, but I need to prepare for my meeting with the lawyer. I'll put this in the sink." Lauren picks up her mug.

"You don't have to…" Olivia starts, but Lauren is already there and in the next second she is waving to Olivia and heading out the door.

"I'll call you tomorrow," Olivia yells, but she is not sure if Lauren hears.

LAUREN runs her fingers over the polished wooden desk that separates her from her divorce lawyer. Everything in the room is pristine, like the woman in front of her, who is slim and beautiful and can't be more than a few years older than Lauren. "I want this over with quickly," Lauren says, trying to convey her own authority. "I want it to be as painless as possible. I don't want to hurt him. I just want him to pay me back and return my valuables."

The lawyer smiles, raising her eyebrows which are perfectly shaped. "That's very noble of you. Let's hope your husband is willing to be equally reasonable." She twirls a strand of hair round her finger. "I'm all for reaching an amicable settlement, but if things don't go to plan I want you to know I will get you the best possible result… financially, I mean."

"Thank you," Lauren says, shifting uncomfortably in her seat. "It should be okay. He's a decent guy."

"Well you know him better than I do," the lawyer concedes. She flicks through the paperwork on her desk. "It's lucky you don't have kids. That makes everything a hundred times harder."

"Yeah really lucky," Lauren mutters, making no effort to disguise the irony in her voice.

OLIVIA hops up and down like an injured animal, grasping at her throbbing toe. "Why would you leave that there?" she yelps, gesturing at a box of Benji's belongings, mostly unidentifiable gadgets, which is lying in the middle of their cramped bedroom.

"Where would you like me to leave it?" he asks from the bed, not looking up from his newspaper.

"Somewhere I won't walk into it!" She hobbles towards him, feeling him laughing at her. "I'm not pretending. It really hurts."

"Sorry Liv, but it's not like I've got any wardrobe space here," he says accusingly, reigniting the argument they've been having for the past few days. "I don't know what you thought would happen when I gave up my flat."

She shoots him a look of disgust. "You don't even care that I hurt myself."

"Of course I care," he sighs, putting down the paper and opening his arms to receive her. "Come here and I'll kiss it better."

"No thanks," Olivia snaps, sitting on the end of the bed and rubbing her toe even though it has stopped hurting. "You should take some of this stuff to your parents' house. They have plenty of room." It's not the first time she's made this suggestion and Benji rolls his eyes upon hearing it again.

"Or you could throw out half your clothes and then I'd have some storage space." He picks up his paper and disappears behind it.

"Don't be ridiculous Benji," Olivia scolds. "As if I don't need them!" She hears him exhale loudly like he always does when he stops engaging and she climbs back into bed, defeated, and whimpering. "I hate it when we fight."

"It's not a real fight," Benji whispers, dropping the paper and smiling at her. He leans in, cupping her face in his hands. "Don't be scared Liv. I'm not going anywhere." He kisses her gently. "You'd honestly have to file a restraining order."

She pulls away, staring at the ceiling, wondering if it might hold the answer to the question that's been plaguing her for days. "But what if we're like Lauren and Ryan?"

Benji laughs out loud. "Are you serious? Of course we're nothing like them. They never liked each other and we've been best friends forever."

"I suppose that's true," she concedes, his reassurances going some way towards quelling her rising panic. "Do you think we need a bigger flat though?

"Probably," he snorts.

JULIA packs her breast pump in her bag and asks Mathis once again if it's really okay for her to go, even though she knows the flight is non-refundable. He promises her they'll be fine and tells her not to cry as she kisses Claude goodbye. "You'll be home in 48 hours," he says. "The time will fly."

She takes the train to the airport, unable to shake the feeling she's forgotten something important as her arms twitch uncomfortably. When she steps onto the platform, wondering if she should turn around and take the next train home, a man with a beard asks if she is lost. She tells him she is fine, at once afraid of what might happen if she doesn't keep going.

The plane is on time and she straps herself into her window seat, which is above the wing. Looking out onto the runway, she imagines what might happen to Claude if she were to die in a crash, then berates herself for thinking such negative thoughts. She doesn't realise she is crying until the old lady beside her pulls a tissue from her bag. "Why are you sad?" she asks in French, offering it to Julia.

"I just miss my baby," Julia explains, accepting the tissue.

"How long are you away for?" the woman enquires, her lined face full of sympathy.

"Only two days," Julia says, imagining how pathetic this must sound.

"I understand. I've raised four kids. The first time you leave them is the hardest," she says, smiling at Julia. Her kindness makes Julia cry a little more; it reminds her of her own mother, who she hasn't seen in months though she has needed her like never before.

LAUREN sits cross-legged on the sofa, unwilling to encroach on the space Ryan used to claim for himself. Still in her yoga pants, she waits for her chamomile tea to cool, while half watching a new reality show which is already irritating her. The autumn light is fading fast, though it has been unusually dark all day, the forecast warning there are storms on the way. Lauren used the meteorological threat as her excuse, when, a couple of hours earlier, she turned down the chance to go out with a group of single friends. These friends had all but disappeared from her life until they heard about her impending divorce, when they magically resurfaced, unable to hide their glee at recruiting a new member to their pack. Lauren knows she needs them; the dinner party invitations have dried up completely, her former, coupled-up friends dropping her before they could be contaminated by her misfortune. With the first roar of thunder she imagines their houses being struck by lightning, a thought she isn't sorry for because it's what they deserve.

Later, when she begins to feel sleepy, she carries her empty mug back through to the kitchen, where the rain is pelting against its sloping windows. The noise is so great she doesn't hear the banging on the front door, but when she returns to the hall she sees it rattle with every thump. Adrenaline pumps through her veins as she recognises she could be in danger; any number of people could be chasing Ryan, or chasing her, for money. Dashing back to the lounge she grabs her phone from beside the sofa, punching in 999 and allowing her finger to hover above the call button. She returns to the hall, to the desperate pounding, and for the first time hears him shouting above the howls of the storm. Dropping her phone she runs to the door, attaching the latch before opening it an inch. "Ryan, what are you doing here?" she yells.

"Lauren please let me in. I didn't know where else to go." His fingers creep though the gap.

She backs away. "Ryan, are you drunk? You can't just turn up here. We're getting divorced."

"Lauren, my dad is sick again, really dying this time. They said his heart is failing." He is sobbing, soaked to the bone and shaking, she can see this now and she unhooks the latch, allowing him to step inside. Her instinct is to hold him and she doesn't fight it.

"Ryan I'm so sorry," she whispers, cradling his head in her arms. "I'm so so sorry. I had no idea."

"He collapsed yesterday. I had to call the ambulance. I've only just left the hospital because they said I should go home and rest." His eyes plead with her. "I didn't know where else to go. I just had to be with you."

"It's okay," she says softly, "I'll always be here for you." Then he kisses her with a need so great she can't say no.

JULIA's clothes are drenched by the time she reaches the small terraced house her parents have inhabited for the past 35 years, a house that looks more tired every time she visits, much like her parents. Her mother is waiting by the front door and throws herself at Julia. She squeezes her until she can barely breathe, before holding her at arm's length to scold her. "How could you come home without the baby? What kind of a daughter does that to her mother? It's cruel, just cruel." Were it not for the twinkle in her mother's eye, Julia might actually believe herself to be in real trouble.

"I told you I'm here to see Lauren...," Julia begins to explain, but the incensed look on her mother's face instantly cuts her off.

"You'd think Lauren was the Queen of England the way you run to her. I've never seen anything like it." Her mother sighs with exasperation. "At least you're here. Come on in. I've made you a cup of tea." She picks up a mug from the decorative church pew in the hallway and hands it over to Julia.

"Thanks," Julia says accepting the drink and taking a sip. "It's ice cold!"

"I made it an hour ago," her mother admits without a hint of an apology. "You were late. You can put it in the microwave. I think your dad's fallen asleep in front of the telly, but you can wake him. I'm going to put dinner on. It's spaghetti Bolognese."

"Great!" Julia abandons her cold tea and wanders into the front room where she finds her father asleep as promised. She strokes his thinning grey hair and he opens his eyes.

"You're home," he smiles, reaching up to touch her face. "My baby is home." She helps him to the table, listening to him complain about the price of petrol and the new neighbours. She waits for him to ask about Claude, but he doesn't; he'd never tell her he was disappointed in her, but she feels it all the same.

The next morning she opens her eyes to the frontman of her favourite band and original love of her life, in the form of a poster looming large above her single bed. Her room hasn't been touched in over a decade and continues to bear the hallmarks of her teenage years. Getting up, she studies the pin board above her desk, littered with ticket stubs from her cinema trips with Olivia: *Donnie Darko*, *Lost in Translation*, *Eternal Sunshine of the Spotless Mind* – how she loved them all, and yet she can't remember the last time she lost herself in a film. The shelves her father once nailed to her wall still house the texts she studied for A-level; biographies of history's greatest tyrants sit alongside English literature's most celebrated classics. It astonishes her now, how she used to devour these books. As she scans the titles, she spots an old photo album poking out the bottom shelf. She reaches for it, sitting back down on her bed to flick through the evidence of her rock climbing on a compulsory school trip (Mathis didn't believe her when she told him) and the pictures from a Halloween house party where her friends convinced her, beyond doubt, she'd seen an actual ghost. She laughs at her own naivety, wishing she had more time to spend with her memories, but knowing Lauren is waiting.

LAUREN is woken by the doorbell, which is being rung with great urgency. "Shit," she cries, sitting bolt upright. "Julia's here. I forgot she was coming." Ryan groans, still half asleep beside her. She shakes him until he opens his eyes. "What should I do?"

"Don't tell her I'm here," he orders, jumping out of bed. "I'll go out the back." He grabs his jeans and jumper, which Lauren left to dry on the radiator, and begins to dress.

"But are you going to be okay?" Lauren asks watching him, his body a little thinner than she remembers.

"Yes," he smiles. "I do feel better today. You'd better let Julia in." The doorbell buzzes again and Lauren dashes to the window overlooking her driveway. The wooden frame has stiffened in the damp weather, but she forces it open, shouting down, "I'll be there in a minute Jules. Sorry. I overslept!" Julia gives her the thumbs up and she closes the window again, for fear Julia might hear something.

When she turns Ryan is fully dressed and hovering by the door. "Lauren, I don't think we should tell anyone about this. I mean we shouldn't tell anyone we've seen each other."

His words unnerve her and she immediately feels like a fool; she'd already imagined making the announcement. "But shouldn't I go see your dad? Shouldn't I at least call your mother?" she asks, her sense of duty, if nothing else, compelling her to argue. "I feel like I should help."

Ryan presses his lips together, making them disappear, then gives his head a slow, single, shake. "It's just too complicated and they've got enough going on. It's better for you to keep your distance. Let's just keep this between us for now."

"Okay," she agrees, "whatever you think is best." She follows him to the top of the staircase. "I'm always here if you need me Ryan."

"I know," he says softly, turning to face her. "Keep Julia in the lounge and I'll sneak out the kitchen in a few minutes."

"Fine." Lauren returns to her bedroom, hearing Ryan pound down the stairs. She throws on her blue skinny jeans and a long-sleeved black t-shirt, regretting not having the time to put an interesting outfit together. Then she ties her hair back in a loose ponytail and wonders if she might tell Julia anyway.

"So so sorry about that!" Lauren says, doing her utmost to sound mortified as she opens the front door to her friend.

"Please don't apologise," Julia steps inside and embraces Lauren, who feels momentarily self-conscious because she hasn't managed to shower. "I'm so glad you had a lie in. You must have been tired?"

"I guess so," Lauren agrees, ushering her friend inside and wishing she would hurry up as she takes off her furry boots, which are in obvious need of replacing. "Let's sit in the front room. The kitchen's too cold."

"Your place is even more beautiful than in the photographs," Julia beams, sinking into a velvet armchair. "Does it feel strange living here on your own?"

Lauren shrugs. "Ryan was hardly here anyway. He was always working," she pauses, remembering again, "or gambling I suppose." She walks to the fireplace, pointing out the photo of Claude she has placed above it, hoping to draw Julia's attention away from both the front window and the details of her marriage.

Julia's eyes light up immediately. "You framed it! He's so much bigger now, you wouldn't believe it."

"Shame you couldn't bring him with." Lauren watches Ryan scurry down the path to the street, feeling herself breathing easy again. "It was really good of you to come Jules."

"I wanted to be here," Julia smiles. "You've got me for the whole day. We can do whatever you like."

"Let's start with breakfast," Lauren suggests, guilt washing over her as she realises how long a whole day with Julia actually sounds. "It's such a shame Liv is away this weekend. I know how much she wanted to see you too."

OLIVIA tosses the plastic wrapper to the floor of the Volkswagen and sinks her teeth into a thick piece of liquorice. They've been sitting in North Circular traffic for what feels like an eternity and Olivia has tired of talking.

"Cheer up Livvy. Once we get through Hanger Lane we should move more quickly," Benji says, reading her mood.

"I'm just so bored," she yawns. "Can't you put the radio on or something?" He obliges, fiddling with the dials on his dashboard. "Not this station," she groans, when Magic FM starts blaring through the speakers.

"I'm changing it. Have some patience," Benji snaps. "There, Radio 1, for you and the other teenagers." Olivia says nothing more, though in her head she is wondering how they got here and how she can find Benji, of all people, so utterly irritating.

"I need the loo. Can we stop?" she asks, when they are finally on the motorway.

"Really Livvy?" Benji sighs. "Didn't you go before we left?"

"I didn't need it then and you don't need to be a prick about it. Just stop at the next services," she orders, scraping her nails across the dashboard.

"Fine." He throws his head back. "No offence, but you're the most annoying person in the world."

"I feel the same about you," she teases, laughing, then regretting it as her urge to wee becomes stronger.

"Well it must be love." He says this so casually she could easily have missed it, keeping his eyes on the road so he can't see the look on Olivia's face, which she's certain would hurt him more than her silent response. "We're almost at the service station," Benji announces, changing lanes, "and you don't have to have a nervous breakdown because I suggested we love each other."

JULIA skips up the stairs, heart almost bursting with longing for her baby. "Come to Mummy," she says softly, when she is finally back inside the apartment, but he clings to his father. "He's forgotten me!" she cries.

"Don't be silly. He's missed his mummy. He's just woken up, that's all," Mathis says, as he continues to cradle the baby. He kisses Julia on the lips. "I have missed you too."

"Let me try again," she demands, stroking Claude's hair. "I want to hold him." The baby buries his face in Mathis's chest and starts to cry, only stopping when she backs away. "He hates me. He actually hates me."

As the hours pass Julia tries, time and again, to feed Claude, but he fusses and rejects her milk. When she sings to him, he squirms in her arms and when she tickles him, he refuses to laugh. She watches Mathis rock her baby to sleep, realising she has become a stranger to him. When she cries to Mathis, he assures her it will be different in the morning, when he goes to work and she is alone with Claude again. "You can't go," she sobs, "not unless he's okay with me."

Mathis is right. Upon waking up, Claude is *her* baby again, and Julia feels the relief of knowing her punishment is over. She kisses his hands, berating herself for being foolish enough to think Lauren needed her more than her own child.

Chapter Seven

LAUREN climbs out of bed, still dizzy with sleepiness as she reaches for her mobile phone. She never knows when to expect him; he calls without warning, letting her know he's outside.

"Hello," she says groggily, rubbing her eyes with her free hand. "I'll come let you in." She already knows tonight will be no different, knows they won't talk about what's happening and knows that when he passes out she'll lie awake wondering why it feels so completely different from before. It is different. There are no dinners, no discussions about what they're doing at the weekend, no days in this new relationship with Ryan at all. They have only the nights, dark nights filled with need and devoid of difficult conversations. She doesn't know what to tell the divorce lawyer. She's been avoiding her calls.

When Ryan leaves the next morning, Lauren pulls the strands of hair from her brush, extracting far more than usual. Flopping back onto her bed, she scrolls through the new messages on her phone, finding a text from a friend wanting to set her up, really pushing her to say yes, like they all are, insisting it's time to move on. She scrolls on, reading a message from Olivia inviting her round for sushi takeway. She accepts the offer; it's the best she's had in a while.

Later, Lauren heads to Belsize Park directly from work, grateful not to be returning to her home and the uncertainty it harbours. She has already placed her order for food and when Olivia opens the door in her pyjamas she assures her dinner will be there soon. Once inside, Lauren removes her heavy coat, already too hot.

"Sorry, let me move those clothes," Olivia says, shifting a pile from the sofa to the floor. "Sit down. I'll get the wine."

Lauren does as instructed, unable to fathom how a relationship can survive in such a confined space. "How's it going with Benji?" she asks.

"It's a learning curve for sure." Olivia hands Lauren a large glass of red wine. "I mean it's harder. It's harder than before. Being in a relationship is hard work. I didn't expect it to be. Sometimes I wonder if I was better off when I was single. Really I do."

"You weren't," Lauren scoffs. "You and Benji were always meant to be together."

"I guess we'll see about that," Olivia sighs, giving way to an uncomfortable silence, which is only broken when the delivery man arrives. "Shit! I need a pound to tip him," Olivia cries, jumping up.

"I've got. Help yourself," Lauren offers, reaching into her bag for her wallet and chucking it at Olivia, who catches it effortlessly.

***

"Please have more," Olivia insists when Lauren puts down her chopsticks signalling she's done. They split the remaining salmon sashimi between them. "I need to get a loyalty card for this place," Olivia jokes. "I must order from them three times a week, basically every time Benj is out."

"Where's he tonight?" Lauren asks, realising she'd forgotten to enquire, though reasoning his absence is the reason for her invite. She was the same, before, and she doesn't blame Olivia for using her in this way.

"He's with the boys." A sheepish look spreads across Olivia's face as she picks at the leftover pieces of ginger. "I think he's seeing Ryan."

"It's okay," Lauren says softly, surprised at the steadiness of her own voice. "I don't expect Benji to drop Ryan as a friend because of me. I mean he's been through a lot and he needs his friends around him too."

"He seems to be doing okay." Olivia raises a single eyebrow, a look Lauren knows well.

"Tell me!" Lauren demands, feeling her chest tighten.

"Okay," Olivia agrees, "but only because if it was me I'd want to know." She inhales sharply. "Benj thinks he's seeing someone. I mean he's sure of it. He says he's been slipping off to meet someone when they've been out together. He's no idea who she is."

"That's none of my business," Lauren snaps, knocking a small tub of soy sauce, which leaks over the coffee table. "Sorry."

"It's fine. Leave it." Olivia gestures for her to sit back down and dabs at the sauce with her own napkin. "I just thought maybe you should know so you feel okay about seeing other people too."

"It's completely unrelated." Lauren folds her arms, furious with Olivia for becoming one of *them*. "You know his dad is really sick?" She doesn't know why she says this; it just comes out.

"I'd not heard." Olivia's face drops and Lauren already knows she has said too much. "Benj hasn't mentioned anything. Are you sure? I really think he would've told Benj."

"He's seriously, seriously ill," Lauren says softly. "He's dying. Ryan came over to tell me. He was a total mess."

"So you've seen him?" Olivia asks, though there is caution in her voice.

"Just a few times," Lauren confesses, "just because he was upset."

She watches the tears roll down Olivia's cheeks and soon she is crying too. "He's lying isn't he? He's a fucking liar."

"He's screwing with the divorce. He's making it harder for you. God knows why, but he is," Olivia says, suddenly appearing animated as if she's landed on the perfect theory. "Do you think it's about money?"

Lauren closes her eyes, picturing the look of satisfaction on Ryan's face that first time she let him in, the morning after the sex, when she told him she'd always be there for him. "I don't think it's that," she says. "I think he's proving he can have what he wants. Think about it. I locked him out the house and filed for divorce, but still he comes round without a word of warning and I give in. I am his. The house is his. He hasn't lost a single thing."

Olivia's face reddens with rage. "Lauren, you'd better make sure that narcissistic fucker gets what he deserves!"

Chapter Eight

JULIA pushes the buggy out her front door and directly into the quiet street in le Suquet, where, just a couple of months ago, she and Mathis had signed the rental agreement on a two bedroom, ground floor apartment and moved in immediately. Her afternoon stroll has become something of a ritual already and she looks forward to it, knowing Claude will sleep for at least an hour giving her enough time to walk to the shore and back. Later, she'll pop over to see Sabine, a mother she met at a play group and with whom she struck up an instant friendship.

For now though, she enjoys the sunshine which is not yet strong enough to feel oppressive, but rather delightfully warming. When she reaches the promenade she is very warm and she stops to buy an ice cream, parking the buggy by a shaded bench so she can sit down to eat it. It's too early in the season for tourists and the oceanfront remains uncluttered and peaceful, a lone sandcastle occupying the beach in front of her. She is imagining building sandcastles with Claude when a gentle hand lands on her shoulder and Julia turns, taking a split second to place his face. "What a surprise!" she squeals. "How are you?"

"I'm great thanks." Greg smiles warmly, his eyes focused on the buggy. "This must be Claude?"

"Yes indeed." Julia feels herself beam with pride as Greg pulls back the sun shade to study her sleeping child.

"Congratulations. He looks so much like you," Greg proclaims, as he looks back and forth between the two of them. "So you're living here now?"

"I am. We just moved. We're not far from the port." Julia realises how excited she sounds, but she can't help it. "Are you here on holiday?" she asks, returning to her ice-cream, which is beginning to melt.

"Just for a couple of weeks. My parents are selling their place, so I'm making the most of it while we still have it," he explains, his bottom lip protruding in a sorry pout.

"Oh that's a shame." Julia licks her spoon.

"Tell me about it," he laughs. "They want a country pad in England now. My mum's sick of flying and she won't drive all this way. Anyway," he looks around, "I wondered if I might see Ryan and Lauren out here again?"

"You won't," Julia says softly. "They're divorcing."

She watches the smile spread across Greg's face. "Really?"

"Really," Julia laughs. "Don't look so happy about it!"

"I'm sorry." His smile fades just a little. "Is Lauren okay?"

"I think she's doing well, but maybe you should call her and find out for yourself?" Julia says this without thinking and immediately feels her cheeks flush red, though Greg doesn't flinch at the suggestion.

"You think she'd be pleased to hear from me?" he asks, stroking his clean shaven chin in contemplation. "Go on then, give me her number. And don't tell her I'm going to call," he warns. "I want her to pick up!"

***

"I already know," Olivia says smugly when she answers the phone. "The boy didn't waste any time."

Julia laughs. "I've been too scared to call. Is Lauren furious with me?"

"Course she is," Olivia teases, "but I'm pretty sure she'll get over it."

The setting sun streams in through the bedroom window and Julia closes her eyes. "I can see it Olivia. I can see the wedding."

"Give me strength!" Olivia cries.

THE END

Printed in Great Britain
by Amazon